Girl Who Freezes Shadows

An Ella Porter Mystery Thriller

Georgia Wagner

Contents

Prologue

The small plane soared through the crisp Alaskan air, slicing through the clouds as it made its descent toward Nome. Inside the aircraft, two men sat side by side, their identical features masked by their impeccably tailored suits. The first man, sporting a three-piece navy blue suit with pinstripes, showcased a striking, gold Rolex watch on his left wrist, its diamond-studded bezel sparkling with every movement. Around his neck hung a thick, platinum chain, featuring a pendant intricately designed with a blend of emeralds and sapphires. On his fingers, he wore several rings, including a magnificent platinum band encrusted with a sizable ruby, which glimmered under the ambient lighting.

Seated next to him, his companion exuded a similarly extravagant aura. He donned a bespoke, charcoal-gray suit, complemented by a crisp, white dress shirt and a vibrant, silk tie adorned with an intricate paisley pattern. A platinum Cartier Santos timepiece graced his wrist, its sapphire blue dial perfectly harmonizing with his ensemble.

1

The jeweled luxury extended all the way down to the handles of their gold-plated Glocks, visible in their etched leather holsters.

An outside observer wouldn't have taken long to realize these two men were brothers.

Twins. And their tanned skin spoke of an existence spent basking in the sun of distant paradises. But their appearances belied their true intentions.

The older brother, Victor, gripped the control stick with a confident hand, guiding the plane toward the isolated runway of Nome's small airport. His sharp gaze darted between the instrument panel and the white expanse of snow below. The younger brother, Vincent, the mirrored reflection of his sibling, kept a watchful eye on the surroundings, his senses attuned to any sign of danger.

As the plane touched down, the roar of the engines subsided, giving way to the eerie stillness of the Arctic wilderness. The brothers exchanged a brief glance, a silent affirmation of their purpose. They didn't speak.

They rarely did.

The two of them had spent their lives together... had lived together and killed together for decades.

In fact, Victor remembered the first time he'd seen a dead man had been in his brother's bedroom when the two of them had only been thirteen.

GIRL WHO FREEZES SHADOWS

It certainly hadn't been the last corpse he'd seen.

Victor glanced at his brother, tapping the side of his time piece, careful not to smudge the glass. Vincent glanced over, then nodded a single time. He turned his phone, showing a smiling face on the screen. An attractive image of an attractive young FBI agent. Blonde hair, an upturned, celestial nose. Blue eyes. There was a stubbornness in those eyes that belied her amicable smile. Her name was Eleanor Porter.

Or, as they thought of her, the target.

The next piece in a long succession of pieces.

A piece of their favorite game.

Victor allowed himself a small, pleasurable smile, like the leer of some crocodile.

They were here to eliminate Ella Porter, a woman who had pried too deeply into the secrets of the game they played. And anyone who knew her would not be spared... proven by the way his brother was now scrolling through other images.

A man. Two women. The brother hesitated on the image of the second woman as the plane bounced and jounced, rolling along the tarmac of the airstrip. Piloting the plane one-handed came naturally to the more experienced twin.

Both brothers leaned in slightly—for their normally reserved selves, this was the equivalent of a gasp of surprise.

The third picture was identical to Ella's.

A twin.

Both men smiled.

This *would* be fun.

Stepping out onto the tarmac, the brothers' presence was immediately conspicuous amidst the desolate landscape. Their opulent attire clashed with the rugged environment, their expensive jewelry glinting under the pale winter sun. Victor adjusted the collar of his tailored overcoat, a barrier against the biting cold, while Vincent straightened the cuffs of his cashmere-lined gloves.

They were not accustomed to such harsh conditions, yet they adapted seamlessly. Their years of experience had honed their abilities to survive in any environment, be it a tropical paradise or a frozen wasteland. But their survival skills extended far beyond the mere physical.

As they moved toward the terminal building, a lone airport worker approached them, his curiosity evident in his eager stride. The man's weathered face creased with lines, a testament to years spent in the unforgiving Arctic climate. He wore multiple layers of clothing, his hands covered by thick gloves.

"Welcome to Nome!" the airport worker greeted, his voice tinged with genuine interest. "I don't often see such well-dressed folks around here. What brings you to our humble town?"

Victor stepped forward. His eyes fixated on the man, and as was often the case, something in his gaze gave the fellow pause. A coldness like the glare of a shark.

The airport worker coughed delicately. "I, er... I couldn't help but notice the plane." The worker smiled vaguely, licking his lips.

Victor watched him.

"Just... just..." The man's breath plumed on the air.

The two twins remained motionless, staring.

"Just..." The airport worker glanced down at a palm pilot then up again. "Your plane... It was, er, reported stolen a couple days ago." He gave a little giggle, trying to deflate tension that only he was feeling.

"Not stolen," said Victor simply, and his voice croaked like the hinge of some ancient tomb being disturbed for the first time in centuries.

The airport worker's eyes gleamed with curiosity. "Oh? So... you're the owners then? Great! Mind showing me the registration?"

Both twins just stared at him. Victor adjusted his sunglasses, and yet his eyes remained unblinking behind the frames. In his line of work, they'd done terrible things to men who asked too many questions. They were well up the leaderboards with the Collective.

"I see... So, er... what are you two here for, then?"

The man definitely seemed less friendly all of a sudden.

"Business," Victor said, his voice as cold as the snow on the distant mountains facing the small airfield.

"What kind of business?"

Vincent, always attuned to his surroundings, noticed a glint of fear in the man's gaze. He knew they couldn't afford to arouse suspicion. With a swift motion, he removed a wad of cash from his pocket, the sight of it enough to capture the airport worker's attention.

The airport worker's eyes widened, his nosy nature piqued by the allure. He hesitated, staring at the cash.

Victor waved it, allowing the crisp bills to flutter in the breeze, diverting the man's attention away from his brother.

As the airport worker stared at the cash, he didn't notice Vincent moving surreptitiously behind him. Vincent was glancing towards the main building. But the small airfield was unmanned save for this single soul. They'd check, of course.

After this business was done.

Now, Vincent had moved to flank. The airport worker's back was exposed to him. Victor didn't speak, didn't gesture; it was like some quiet telepathy passed between them. Victor moved the wad of cash, extending it towards the worker.

The airport attendant hesitated.

And then, with swift, calculated movements, Vincent closed the distance, his gloved hand pulling a flash of silver from inside his sleeve.

The airport worker didn't even have time to react, to croak, to scream.

One moment, he'd been standing, greedily eyeing the cash, the next, he stiffened as Vincent slid a gleaming blade across the worker's throat.

A startled gasp escaped the man's lips as crimson blood spurted from the fatal wound. His eyes widened in disbelief, the shock of his impending death etched across his face.

Victor and Vincent didn't react.

With cold efficiency, Vincent withdrew the blade, leaving the airport worker to crumple to the ground, his life rapidly slipping away. Victor, never breaking his stride, glanced back briefly at the dying man, his gaze devoid of remorse.

Unfazed by the gruesome scene they left behind, the brothers made their way to a Jeep parked discreetly at the edge of the runway. The vehicle had been provided by a local contact, a part of the intricate web of alliances that allowed them to operate with impunity. They climbed into the Jeep, their movements swift and purposeful. Further down the road, stretched along the coast, the town of Nome spread out before them, a desolate yet hauntingly beautiful landscape. The cold wind whipped through the streets, carrying whispers of impending danger.

As they drove into the heart of Nome, the brothers' attention turned to their primary target: an FBI agent. Ella Porter's relentless meddling had threatened to expose them, and for that, she had to pay.

Not to mention... an old friend of theirs had visited her on more than one occasion. The brothers knew that their mission would not end with only her. Anyone who knew her, anyone who could potentially pose a threat, would be eliminated without mercy.

Chapter 1

Ella slowly opened her eyes as the sun streamed through the dusty blinds of Brenner's apartment. She yawned and stretched, noticing the lumpy futon mattress and mismatched sheets. The apartment was sparsely furnished with a small TV on a plywood stand, a couple of folding chairs, and a card table in the corner that served as a desk.

She'd spent the night. A small smile curled her lips as she realized where she was. She could hear Brenner brushing his teeth from the small bathroom in the back of the cramped apartment.

As she lay there, though, other memories came back.

Their conversations last night... well into the night.

She paused, sitting up slowly, a frown cresting her features. They'd talked about far more than just their relationship.

A shiver went down her spine. They'd spoken of the Collective. They'd talked about her father, her family...

And they'd talked about Mortimer Graves, the Graveyard Killer. The serial killer she'd once allowed to escape from custody.

Another shiver joined the first, tremoring along her arms, raising goosebumps. She glanced once more towards the bathroom, listening to the sound of Brenner brushing his teeth.

His computer screen glowed from the table across the room, where it sat. She stared at it, wondering briefly what Brenner was researching.

She took in a few deep breaths. He was still here. He hadn't left.

After their conversation, he hadn't gone running.

Instead...

Another small smile curled her lips. She glanced over the side of the bed, swinging her legs in the same direction.

She rummaged through her worn backpack for a clean shirt and jeans, wrinkling her nose at the musty smell. Her entire wardrobe consisted of secondhand clothing, bought for a few dollars at the local thrift store. She couldn't remember the last time she bought anything new.

As Ella got dressed, she thought about how she needed to stop at the laundromat on her way into the office. Her tiny apartment didn't have its own washer or dryer, and she refused to pay the fees at the complex's laundry room. She sighed, knowing it would be another long day at the small Bureau field office. At least she'd get to see Brenner again tonight.

Brenner emerged from the bathroom, dressed in his usual jeans and t-shirt. "Want some coffee before you head into work?" he asked.

Ella shook her head. "I should get going. Lots to do today."

"I know the feeling," Brenner said, flashing a quick smile. His eyes didn't seem nearly as sad as they so often did. "Hey, do you need a ride to work or anything? I'm happy to drive you." He hesitated, watching her.

She flashed a quick smile. "You sure know how to treat a woman afterwards."

"After what?" he said with an innocent shrug.

She rolled her eyes and flung a couple of socks at him, which ricocheted off his muscled chest. She could see the faintest outline of a fresh bandage under his t-shirt. He'd taken a bullet for her sister.

But they'd talked about this, too.

"Nah, that's fine. I'll see you tonight, okay?"

Brenner kissed her forehead. "Be careful out there."

For a moment, she didn't move, leaning her head on his chest. His arm was draped around her, holding her close.

She smiled, breathing in his familiar scent of pine and gun oil. How many times had they woken up like this as teenagers? Before everything had fallen apart.

"I can hear you thinking," Brenner rumbled, his voice vibrating through her cheek.

"Just remembering," she said.

His hand stroked down her spine. "Good memories, I hope."

"The best." She tilted her head up to meet his gaze. Those glacial blue eyes stared down at her, filled with a tenderness that made her heart skip. "I'm glad we found our way back to each other."

"Me too, El." His lips quirked. "Took us long enough."

She nudged him with her elbow, unable to hold back a grin. "Whose fault was that?"

"Yours, of course." But his teasing tone took any sting from the words. "You were the one who ran off to Quantico."

"And you were the one who didn't ask me to stay," she shot back. An old argument, worn smooth with time.

He sobered, brushing a strand of hair from her face. "The past is in the past."

It was as she spoke that she glanced past him and hesitated. Now that he'd moved, she had a better view of the search bar on the laptop.

She paused. "You're looking them up?"

"Hmm?"

"The federal database. You're looking for the Collective?"

He glanced down at her, distancing a bit to get a good look. "You saying I shouldn't?"

She shook her head. "No..." She frowned, troubled. "Did you find anything?"

"Not yet." Frustration edged his tone. "There's no trace of them anywhere. No digital footprint, no financials, no known members or locations. It's like they don't exist." Brenner grimaced, scrubbing a hand over the stubble lining his jaw.

"Or we're not looking in the right places," Ella said, pinching the bridge of her nose. "There has to be something. Some clue we've missed."

"You're sure this is real?"

"I told you last night."

"I was a bit distracted."

"Right... Priscilla confirmed it. My dad had a file on them. They're real."

"A country club for killers," said Brenner. "Sounds like a bad horror movie."

She sighed, slumping against him. "I know. I just wish it didn't feel like we were chasing ghosts."

"Ghosts can't hide forever." He stroked a thumb along the inside of her wrist, feeling her pulse beat steady under his touch

Then she straightened, a new light entering her eyes. Determination. Resolve. "You're right. Let's go back to the drawing board."

"Where do you want to start?" he asked.

She stared at the laptop for a long moment, gears visibly turning in her mind.

"The Collective's money has to go somewhere," she said at last. "Every organization needs funding. If we can find where their money is moving, that might lead us to them."

Brenner nodded. "Worth a shot. But whose financials do we start with?"

Ella glanced at him. Winced. Then said, "Maybe my dad? He has ties to this somehow." Ella rose to her feet, cracking her knuckles. "I'll go over the case files again, see if there's anything we missed. We'll get them, Brenner. One way or another."

As she spoke, her excitement mounting, they were suddenly interrupted.

A sharp knock rattled the apartment door. He and Ella glanced at each other, confusion etched on both their faces. Ella paused, glanced at her phone which she'd left on the nightstand, and then a cold, dull dread filled her soul.

It was as if she could see *through* the door to the soul beyond.

Or, at least, where there *should* have been a soul.

"He said he was coming. He wanted to talk in person..." She murmured.

"What?" Brenner asked.

Before she replied, he rose, limping over to the door. Cautiously, he peered through the peephole—and froze.

Ella came up next to him and also peered out.

A prim, properly-dressed man stood outside, hands folded before him. Pale skin, neatly combed brown hair, and wire-framed glasses perched on the bridge of his nose. The very picture of a mild-mannered English gentleman.

But Ella knew better. Knew those placid features and placating smile hid something dark. Something sinister.

Mortimer Graves had come calling.

Brenner's hand curled into a fist. Beside him, Ella sucked in a sharp breath.

The serial killer rapped his knuckles against the door again, the picture of politeness. "Ms. Porter? I was hoping we could have a word." His voice held the barest hint of an English accent, cultured and smooth.

Ella noticed Brenner trembled with the apparent effort not to throw open the door and pummel that smug face. He gritted his teeth, glaring through the peephole. "What do you want?"

"Merely to talk," Mortimer said. "Is that the voice of Marshall Gunn I recognize?"

"The only business I have with you involves putting you in handcuffs," Brenner growled. His fingers curled around the doorknob. He didn't fling it open, though. Ella knew Brenner was a strategic type. He was likely checking to see if Graves had come with backup.

Ella placed a hand on his arm, stilling him.

Brenner straightened, squaring his shoulders. He cast one last glare at Mortimer through the peephole. "Get lost," he snapped. "We've got nothing to say to each other."

Mortimer's placid smile didn't waver. But for a brief moment, his eyes glinted behind those wire-framed glasses. A cold, predatory light. "Eleanor reached out to me, Mr. Gunn."

Brenner shot her a look. She flinched but nodded. "I was asking him about *them*," she whispered.

"This is the guy, though?" Brenner whispered. "Your fake CI?"

Ella flinched at the note of injury in his tone. She'd lied to him about Mortimer. And last night, the conversation about who he really was, what she'd done by letting him escape... It had taken some time to get through their chat.

But now, Brenner was tense. She could see the distrust, the fear in his eyes. Suddenly, without warning, Brenner flung the door open.

"Wait!" she called.

But too late. He lunged through the door, fist swinging fast, aimed at Mortimer Graves' head.

Chapter 2

Brenner's fist shot toward Graves' face, fueled by a protective instinct that often seemed to rear its head whenever Ella was involved.

She shouted out, "Bren—don't!"

But in an instant, Graves sidestepped the blow in an impressive shift of body weight. But Brenner also had the instincts of a killer, and in his case, the instincts came with years of military training.

As Graves dodged, Brenner shifted his weight, driving through the doorway, and trying to catch Graves' leg.

The killer stumbled but managed to remain upright, some of his perfectly placed gray hairs now disheveled and out of place.

For a moment, as Ella stared, eyes wide, the two men glared at each other.

Graves was breathing slowly, hinting at impressive cardio for a man of his age.

"Really, Brenner? Is that how we're doing this?" Graves said, his gaze meeting Brenner's in a challenge. Strangely, to Ella's mind, Graves didn't look angry so much as calculating.

The tension in the air was palpable, like the static charge before a storm. Brenner's eyes narrowed as he sized up Graves, assessing his next move. He had always been suspicious of Mortimer, and after their conversation the previous night, he'd clearly made up his mind about the killer.

"Alright then," Brenner muttered with a growl, then he launched himself at Graves with the full force of his muscular frame. The former Navy SEAL's agility was evident as he aimed to tackle him to the ground.

But Graves, ever the cunning adversary, anticipated Brenner's attack. With swift grace, he sidestepped the charge and used Brenner's own momentum to allow the ex-SEAL to careen into the wall.

Ella glimpsed something then, even as she moved to try and snatch at Brenner's shirt, to drag him back. In that instant, she spotted Graves, his eyes gleaming with a wild excitement that sent chills down Ella's spine. She could practically taste the acerbity, as acrid as burnt coffee on her tongue.

Brenner rolled to his feet and lunged at Graves again. Ella only managed to snag at his arm but failed to hold him back. The two men became a blur of fists and kicks, each man unleashing honed skills in a desperate struggle for dominance.

Ella knew she couldn't let this continue. As an FBI agent, she had learned to handle tense situations—but this was personal. With a rush of adrenaline, she stepped between the two men, pale blue eyes blazing with determination.

Ella's muscles tensed as she prepared to separate the two men, her eyes darting between their flushed faces and clenched fists. They had hesitated as she emerged between them, clearly not wanting to harm her in their desire to lash out at each other.

She could see that the fight was far from over, and time was ticking. Taking a deep breath, she mustered every ounce of strength within her and shoved Brenner and Graves apart with a force that surprised even herself.

"Stop!" she cried even louder, her voice sharp and commanding. Her pale blue eyes flashed like ice as she glared at both men, daring them to challenge her authority.

Brenner stumbled back, his gaze never leaving Graves. The fire in his eyes burned just as fiercely as before, but he held his ground, unwilling to defy Ella any further.

Graves, however, frowned in irritation, rubbing his jaw where a bruise was already beginning to form. "Bloody hell," he muttered under his breath, glaring daggers at Brenner. "I didn't come here for this."

Ella's heart raced as she stood between them, her chest heaving with exertion. She could feel the chill of the Alaskan air lingering on her skin, coming through a cracked window at the end of the apartment hallway, the cold seeping through the fabric of her clothing. The scent of damp earth and pine filled her nostrils, wafting in from the small creek outside.

"Neither did I," she whispered, her breath fogging up in the suddenly chilly, hallway air. "But we can't let our suspicions and personal grudges get in the way of what's important."

"Putting him in the ground *feels* important," Brenner muttered.

"I'd like to see you take your best shot," Graves retorted, smirking.

"Please, stop!" she commanded, her voice cutting through the fray like a knife. The sound of her command echoed in the apartment hallway, and for a moment, the world seemed to stand still.

Brenner went quiet again, glancing at her. Graves still remained poised, attentive, watchful, and briefly—it seemed—eager to continue the fracas. Both men had paused their attempts to reach each other past her, though, breathing heavily as they acknowledged her. It was clear that neither wanted to back down, but Ella knew she had to defuse the situation.

Nervously, she glanced towards the two other apartment doors dotting the hallway, making sure no one was peering out at them.

"Enough!" she demanded, the authority in her voice unwavering. "We don't have time for this. Brenner, I called Graves. He's here to *help* us."

Brenner's chest heaved as he stared at Ella, his blue eyes searching hers for any sign of doubt. But her resolve was steadfast, and eventually, he just shrugged, massaging at his knuckles, stepping back. He jammed a thumb towards Mortimer. "Asshole is packing."

Ella blinked. Graves flashed his cold, crocodile smile, and he pulled his jacket away to reveal a sidearm holstered at his waist.

"Concealed, I thought," Graves said, nodding appreciatively. "Nice eye," he complemented Brenner as if the two of them had simply been on a casual stroll rather than a fist fight.

Graves slowly adjusted his charcoal-gray suit sleeves, smoothed his hair back into place, then addressed Brenner. "I can see you know a bit more about me this time around, hmm?"

"I told him what I know," Ella cut in stiffly.

"I see. Well... would you like me to tell you what *I* know?" He quirked an eyebrow.

Ella tensed. Brenner was still breathing heavily and glaring at Graves, but after a moment, Brenner shot Ella a look, searching her gaze as if to say *are you sure?*

She sighed, nodding once.

Then, Brenner stepped back into his apartment, keeping himself between Ella and Mortimer Graves.

The serial killer smoothed the front of his suit, and then one of his leather, stitched penny loafers entered the room as he followed them.

The door closed behind him with a quiet *click.* In fact, much of Graves' movement seemed quiet, sure-footed, and graceful.

They reached the kitchen table, where Brenner remained standing as Ella took a seat.

Graves remained by the fridge, arms crossed.

Brenner said, "Alright. You came to talk. So talk."

"And what I have to say, you're sure you want to hear?" Graves murmured, his eyes hooded now. "Once you hear it, there is no going back." He swallowed briefly then paused, frowned, and held up a finger.

He fished his phone from his pocket, hesitated, and muttered, "One second."

Then he turned towards the blank wall by the fridge. In fact, most of Brenner's walls were blank. Finally, Graves said in a soft voice, "Hey, buddy, daddy's working, mind if I call you back in a few, sport? Mhmm..." A little laugh. "Way to go! That's incredible. You scored twice?" Another laugh. Then, a brief, sweet farewell, and the phone was hung up. Graves turned back around then, glancing at the two figures by the kitchen table.

The smile on his face and the treacle sweet tone vanished to be replaced by a mask.

Ella had often wondered about these brief snippets of calls she'd overheard from Graves, but she had long ago realized the less she pried into this man's personal life, the better.

"Well," Graves said casually, "Are you sure you want to stay and listen, Mr. Gunn?"

"Yes." Brenner didn't add anything else. Didn't pause to consider it. Just a single nod and a single syllable.

"Wouldn't expect anything less," said Mortimer, his gaze lingering on Ella before he turned to face Brenner once more.

Ella could feel the weight of their stares upon her now but she refused to waver. She had a job to do, and she wasn't going to let personal conflicts stand in her way. Her heart raced with anticipation, knowing that every moment counted in their search for answers.

As the tension between Brenner and Graves continued to smolder, Ella braced herself for whatever Graves had come to share.

She said, "What's so important that you had to visit in person to tell me?" she said.

His eyes found hers now. Those cold, corpse-gray eyes. "Well," he said softly, "Some things one ought not speak of on unencrypted airwaves."

She wrinkled her nose. "The phone call? You don't think they're monitoring me, do you?"

Graves shrugged. "If you've been looking into them, then they know about you."

"Them? The Collective?" Brenner cut in. "It's just a bunch of sick twists? Like some murder cult?"

Graves hesitated, shrugging one shoulder. "Perhaps one way to describe them. But there is no *just* about them. Nothing to minimize what they are or the influence they have.

Graves shot a hesitant glance over his shoulder towards the door, as if double-checking it was still closed. Then he sighed. "So be it," he muttered. "I didn't come all this way for something that isn't important. Once I tell you... things will change. They'll know. And then they'll come."

Ella hid the frown creeping across her features. She took a steady breath, then said, "Why don't you start at the beginning?"

Chapter 3

Graves straightened up, brushing at his clothes with an air of annoyance, though his suit was immaculate and Ella spotted no debris of any sort. Ella watched as his fingers methodically tapped away at some imaginary specks of grime from his pristine attire. He was clearly irked by the altercation with Brenner, but his gestures signaled a begrudging willingness to proceed with their discussion.

"Alright," he said from where he stood by the small fridge in the sparse kitchen. Graves leaned in closer towards where Ella sat at the kitchen table, his voice low and laden with an ominous weight. The dimly lit room seemed to tighten its grip.

"You see, Ms. Porter," Graves said softly, watching her with his shark-like gaze, his words as soft as drops of lace. "This group, they operate in the shadows, their presence woven seamlessly into the tapestry of our everyday lives." As Graves spoke, his eyes flickered with a mixture of trepidation and fascination. "But they are far from ordinary. They are the architects of a macabre game, a chilling network of serial killers hidden in plain sight."

Ella just watched. Priscilla had already revealed as much. She said, "Who funds them? Who organizes them?"

"A man known only as the Architect," said Graves with a nod. He reached up and brushed his already smooth bangs. "An eccentric billionaire whose identity remains veiled, silently pulling the strings from the darkness. His money flows like a river, shrouded in anonymity, fueling the Collective's insidious pursuits."

"If I remember correctly, you have some money to spare of your own," Brenner cut in, frowning at Graves. "A private helicopter too, if I'm not mistaken."

"I come from means but nothing like this obscure figure."

"You know who it is, though," Brenner said. "Don't you?"

Graves sniffed. "No."

Brenner's arms crossed over his chest, and his eyebrows moved low. "So why are you even here, Mort? Why not just tell Ella over the phone? If they're keeping such close tabs, you must know a thing or two about them."

"I've been approached by them," he said simply. "More than once."

"Approached how?" Ella asked.

Graves chuckled, and it was a sound like cracking tombstones. "Once for me to join in their sordid little game. But I don't kill how they kill..." Graves flashed a grin, his teeth white. "I kill men and women like *them*."

27

"You're a good guy serial killer, then?" Brenner asked.

No one replied at first. For a brief moment, Graves glanced at Ella, as if searching her expression for something.

After all, she'd been the one to release him from custody. She'd been the one to find him, after months of failed leads and false starts, she'd been able to locate the killer...

But then she'd found out who he was... what he'd been doing.

The last victim Graves had taken had been a child predator who the authorities had known about, but scant evidence had prevented them from prosecuting him.

In a way, Graves, with his money and violent tendencies, was something of a psychopathic Batman. A vigilante.

But things were all too real, standing there, speaking face to face with a man she'd seen kill.

She swallowed vaguely, shaking her head. "You have to know *something*," she said. "If we can find who funds them, we can find this operation, and close the whole thing down."

"This billionaire, Ella, no one can identify him. He lurks in the shadows, funding their operations, orchestrating this dark symphony," Graves murmured, the weight of the revelation hanging heavily in the air. "And the Collective's games... they are nothing short of a depraved contest. They keep score, you see. Points are awarded for the number of lives extinguished, for the audacity and creativity of their kills."

Ella's mind recoiled. Graves pressed on, his voice a chilling cadence in the stillness of the room.

"Their scores, Ella, they reflect the success of their atrocities. Points are tallied for those who manage to elude capture, who leave no trace behind. And the more challenging the target, the higher the stakes. Just a month ago, I caught wind of a governor's daughter, spirited away from under the watchful eyes of those in power, a gruesome offering to their deranged game," Graves revealed, his voice a dark whisper that seemed to echo. "A governor's daughter would've been worth more esteem in their game of murder. A prostitute on the side of the road? Far less..."

"It... it sounds so... implausible," Ella said, carefully. But she thought of her father's little journal. Of the USB drive she'd discovered. Of her sister's reaction to all of it. In fact, Ella had run into a member of the Collective on a crabbing vessel off the shores of Nome. She knew it was real.

"They are resourced, Ella, their reach extending far beyond the boundaries of reason. This is a group that thrives on darkness, that revels in the perverse artistry of murder. Their existence, concealed from the world, is a testament to their cunning and their capability to evade justice," Graves concluded, his words hanging heavily in the air, leaving Ella with a chilling awareness.

As the weight of the Collective's history settled upon them, the room seemed to exhale a heavy breath, as if the shadows themselves carried the echoes of their sins.

Ella's gaze locked onto Mortimer's, cold yet resolute. She crossed her arms over her chest. "Aren't these the sort of people... you *take care of?*"

Brenner had stiffened at these words, and he was staring at the table where his hand rested. He didn't look up but seemed troubled.

Graves shrugged but didn't reply right away.

Her words hung heavy in the chilly air, mingling with the scent of damp earth and the distant echo of a dog barking somewhere in the night, both due to the open window above Brenner's terrace. Mortimer Graves regarded her with an unreadable expression, his eyes flicking over her face like a predator sizing up its prey.

"Very well," he replied coolly, a hint of intrigue creeping into his tone. "Let us say they are the types that I spend time in pursuit of... There are those who not even I can find."

"You seem scared," Brenner said at last, looking up and raising an eyebrow as if challenging Mortimer. "Are you?"

Graves frowned at Brenner, but the Marshal didn't look away.

"What I think he means to say," Ella cut in quickly, "Is maybe we have a better chance working together?"

"That's not what I meant to say," Brenner protested.

But Ella continued.

"Because if my suspicions are correct, we're facing something far bigger and more dangerous than any of us realize." Her heart pounded in her chest. "And if you care about your strange form of justice or even just your own survival, judging by your reaction to my simple phone call, then you'll help me get to the bottom of this before it's too late."

She could feel the icy chill of the Alaskan morning seeping through her clothes, raising goosebumps on her arms. Her breath puffed out in crystalline gusts, towards the open window, each exhale a reminder of the urgency of their task. The shadows cast by the balcony light seemed to dance and sway around them as if whispering secrets of their own.

"It is why I'm here. I won't deny it," Graves conceded, his eyes narrowing. "I'll help you. But I want something in return."

Ella's jaw tightened as she waited for him to continue. She knew there would be a price to pay.

"Only... one thing," Graves said softly, looking at her now. "You have to agree to the favor first."

She blinked.

"Before you tell me what it is?"

He nodded.

"I can't do that."

"And yet I suspect you will." He didn't say anything else.

Neither did she.

Brenner just scowled, clearly communicating what he thought of this arrangement in his posture.

Ella hesitated for a moment, her pale blue eyes meeting Graves' in a silent battle of wills. She knew she couldn't trust him completely, but she needed his information. Yet, every fiber of her being screamed at her to be cautious, to stay on guard.

"Time is something we don't have, Graves," she shot back, her voice laced with steel. "So either tell me what you know or get out of my house."

"This is Mr. Gunn's place, isn't it?" Graves said casually, but his words were chosen specifically. He clearly wanted them to know he was keeping tabs.

Graves raised an eyebrow, testing the limits of her patience. But after a moment, he sighed and relented, his expression turning serious.

"Very well," he said, his eyes locking onto hers with an intensity that sent shivers down her spine. "But remember, Agent Porter, I expect to collect on debts. If I help you, I *will* expect a favor in return."

"I've already done you a pretty significant favor, remember?" she retorted. "That backseat of that car? You could easily still be there."

"And I believe I've already repaid that favor by speaking with you," he said, his voice stern.

They all fell silent briefly. And Ella, as she so often did, glanced around, taking in the details surrounding them.

The kitchen was bathed in the soft glow of the early morning sun filtering through sheer curtains, casting dappled patterns onto the worn wooden floors. A round, oak kitchen table stood in the center, surrounded by mismatched chairs that held their own stories and memories. The scent of freshly brewed coffee mingled with the aroma of bacon which Brenner had cooked for himself earlier. The cast iron pan he'd used remained on the stove's back burner.

Suddenly, there was a creaking of a chair as Brenner surged to his feet, scowling.

One of Brenner's fingers was pointed at Graves' smug face.

"How do we know he's not one of them?" Brenner demanded. "What if he was sent here to take you out?"

Graves, however, seemed unfazed by Brenner's accusations. His posture was relaxed, one elbow resting casually on the counter as he swirled some coffee with a spoon that Ella hadn't even realized he'd poured for himself. His voice was steady, betraying no nerves or concern. "I understand your apprehension, Mr. Gunn," he said. "But I assure you that my presence here is not part of some sinister plot."

"Then why are you here?" Brenner demanded, his fingers still tapping the table, his eyes never leaving Graves. "Out of some sense of altruism? You're a killer."

"Not all killers are the same, Mr. Gunn."

"So you're telling me it bothers you that this so-called Collective is stacking bodies?"

"Stacking up body counts is just the beginning," Graves continued, his tone remaining neutral. "They play a dangerous game, competing with one another for power and influence. The more chaos they create, the higher their standing within the group."

Brenner let out a huff of disbelief. "Sounds like something straight out of a conspiracy theory," he muttered, still gripping the table edge tightly. "Next, you're going to tell us they're responsible for Epstein's Island too?"

"Hardly," Graves replied, a hint of amusement in his voice. "Though they share some similarities in their tendencies for secrecy and manipulation, the Collective is far more dangerous. Their connections and resources are vast, and they won't hesitate to use them to achieve their goals. Whether you believe me or not," he said, his voice growing serious as he locked eyes with Ella, "the Collective is very real. And they pose a significant threat to anyone who stands in their way."

Graves leaned in slightly, his eyes never leaving Ella's. "Ella, if you continue to pursue this case, you'll be placing yourself directly in their crosshairs. They won't hesitate to eliminate threats, and your investigation could make you a prime target."

Ella's breath caught in her throat as Graves issued his warning. Her pale blue eyes widened, and her fingers twitched nervously on the table's edge.

"Are you- are you saying I should back off?" she asked hesitantly, her voice barely above a whisper. She tried to ignore the way her heart hammered against her ribcage, the blood rushing in her ears as fear threatened to consume her.

Brenner clenched his jaw, his knuckles turning white against the oak kitchen table. His agitation was palpable, but Ella couldn't help feeling grateful for his unwavering support.

"Listen," Graves said, his voice low and steady. "I'm not telling you to abandon your work, but you need to understand the stakes. If the Collective realizes you're getting too close, they will retaliate. And they won't show mercy."

The air in the kitchen felt heavy, oppressive. She swallowed hard, her mouth suddenly dry. The weight of responsibility settled on her shoulders, an uncomfortable reminder of the danger that loomed just beyond her reach.

Ella glanced at Brenner, seeking reassurance. She found it in the stubborn set of his jaw, the fierce determination that burned in his blue eyes. They were a team—they would face this threat together.

"Alright," she murmured softly, trying to project a sense of confidence she didn't quite feel. "We'll be careful. We'll do whatever it takes to stay one step ahead of them."

"Good," Graves replied, his expression unreadable. "Because once the Collective marks you as a threat, there's no turning back."

Ella nodded, her hands shaking imperceptibly as she pushed herself to her feet. She could feel Brenner's eyes on her, concern etched into every line of his face. But she couldn't afford to dwell on her fear—not when lives were at stake.

"So how do we help each other, then?" she said quietly. "*What* can you tell me?"

"Well... we need to find the Architect, don't we? You were right in mentioning that we ought to follow the funds." He shrugged.

She nodded, giving her agreement. "So how do we do that?"

Ella's heart pounded in her chest as she tried to process the information Graves had shared. The dimly lit kitchen seemed to close in around her, the wooden table and chairs casting eerie shadows on the worn floor. A faint hum emitted from the overhead fluorescent light, adding to the oppressive atmosphere.

Before Graves could reply, though, Ella's phone suddenly began to ring.

She frowned, reaching to put it on silent.

But just then, Brenner's phone began to ring as well.

And a second later, a siren began to echo in the distance.

"Work calls?" Mortimer guessed, smiling at them both.

Ella frowned, glancing at Brenner.

"No matter," Graves said. "I need to do some of my own digging while I'm here, anyway. Go tend to your commitments. We can speak later this evening, once I've found some answers."

Ella wanted to protest, but the phone was still chirping loudly. The distant sirens were now wailing.

Graves didn't bid farewell. He nodded a single time, then slipped seamlessly back out of the apartment door, like oil spilling through a crack.

Just as quickly, he was gone.

At her side, Brenner tensed as if wanting to pursue Graves, but then he settled again, cursed, and answered his phone.

"What?" Brenner demanded. A pause. "Now? Where? Shit. Okay, I'll tell her. On our way."

He looked at Ella, who was still staring at the door.

"Work?" she asked.

"Yeah. Marshals assisting because of the terrain."

Ella hesitated then glanced down at Brenner.

"The *terrain?*"

Brenner grunted as he pushed to his feet. "Yeah. Body found in a glacier. They want us there ten minutes ago. I'll drive."

Chapter 4

The icy wind whipped around Ella, sending chills down her spine as she stood facing the desolate landscape. Her pale blue eyes scanned the quiet surroundings, weighing the decision that lay before her.

"Damn it," she muttered under her breath, her warm breath crystallizing in the frigid air. She clenched her gloved fists.

The early morning sun cast a soft, ethereal glow over the snow-covered landscape of the Mendenhall Ice Caves. With Brenner by her side, they stepped away from their unmarked car and approached the entrance, their breath forming small puffs of vapor in the chilly air. The sound of crunching snow beneath their boots mingled with the distant murmurs of officers and investigators already on the scene.

A group of local police officers, clad in heavy winter gear, greeted Ella and Brenner, their expressions a mix of curiosity and concern. One of the officers, a burly man with a weathered face, raised a hand in greeting, his sun-stained features twisting into a faint frown.

Ella nodded back, but her gaze moved past him.

GIRL WHO FREEZES SHADOWS

One of the most striking aspects of the Mendenhall Ice Caves was their ethereal blue hue. The glacial ice spread across the desolate land carried an otherworldly quality, with shades of turquoise, sapphire, and deep blue. The vibrant color was a result of the ice's dense composition, which absorbed longer wavelengths of light; the interplay of light created an incredible visual spectacle that seemed almost surreal.

As they approached the entrance to the caves, Ella's eyes were taken to the formations within. The ice formations boasted intricate patterns, jagged edges, and smooth curves. The constant movement of the glacier carved stunning features, creating a natural sculpture. Ella had visited before, especially in her youth. In a way, it reminded her of the cases she worked: every corner and crevice of the ice caves held a unique surprise, as if the ice itself was whispering its own tale of centuries-old transformation.

The caves also boasted an extraordinary quality of light. As sunlight filtered through the translucent ice, it created a soft, diffused glow that illuminated the entire space.

Brenner glanced at Ella as they reached the cave, and the two of them spotted more figures scurrying about within.

The Mendenhall Ice Caves were not only visually striking but also acoustically captivating. The dense ice absorbed sound waves, creating a profound stillness within the caves.

As they neared the heart of the icy cavity, Ella's breath caught in her throat. There, amidst the frozen beauty, was a macabre sight that sharply contrasted with the serene surroundings.

The body of a woman, seemingly suspended in a graceful pose, was perfectly preserved within a block of ice. She was dressed in a tattered ballet costume, her arms gracefully arched above her head, resembling a beautiful ballet dancer frozen in time.

Ella studied the body, her eyes sweeping over the details with a mixture of fascination and dread. The woman's delicate features, though pale and lifeless, exuded an ethereal elegance. But what truly caught Ella's attention were the ballet shoes adorning the woman's feet. Ella marveled at the dedication required to pose a lifeless body in such a manner.

"We have an ID?" Brenner called out, waving towards a forensic agent near the body.

The woman glanced over, did a double take, and frowned. "Marshal?" she said.

Ella was briefly taken aback, as Brenner hadn't even flashed ID. But she supposed in this small town, everyone knew everyone.

Brenner just nodded. "They called in all hands," he said with a shrug.

The forensic agent nodded, glancing back at the body, and said, "Yeah. Already identified."

She stepped aside as another woman in a pale lab coat hurried past. A man was standing near another off-shoot tunnel, holding a plastic bag.

The forensic agent was glancing at his phone, frowning, then looked up, turning the phone so they could see. Ella and Brenner both leaned in, studying the information displayed before them.

A smiling face from a DMV photo. Ella frowned, glancing up at the ballerina suspended in ice. She shivered.

"Lily Harding," Ella said softly. "She looks so..." Ella trailed off, glancing back at the DMV photo. Lily Harding was smiling in the photo. The same couldn't be said about where she hung suspended in ice.

"Where was Lily from?" Brenner asked.

"Local," said the techie. "Moved here to live with her aunt a few years ago." He shrugged. "We're still trying to locate the aunt."

"She's missing?" Ella said suddenly.

"No, no, nothing like that. At least, we don't think." The forensic agent shrugged. "Probably at work. She's on one of the gold dredges."

Ella felt a shiver at the word *gold.* Thoughts of her family came circling back.

She frowned and looked towards the ballerina suspended in ice once more.

"How do you think he brought the ice block down here?" Brenner said after a bit, frowning. "Gotta weigh a couple tons."

Ella frowned, scratching at her chin. "Good point," she murmured.

Brenner's words reminded Ella of the enormity of the task at hand. Whoever had done this was methodical, had planned it out, and had chosen their victim with purpose. Ella's mind raced as she surveyed the scene. The ice block was too big to have been brought in without ample equipment, yet there were no signs of machinery or any unusual activity around the cave. The killer had to have been methodical, calculating every step before executing it flawlessly.

Ella's thoughts were interrupted as a radio crackled to life. "Agent Porter?" the voice asked.

Ella held up the device. "This is Porter."

"Agent, we've just gotten word from the dredge. The aunt's there."

Ella's heart sank. It was always harder when family members were involved.

"Alright. We'll head out in a few," she said.

Brenner nodded, already taking the keys out of his pocket. But the quiet jingle of metal distracted Ella as she glanced once more at the body suspended in ice.

Stepping closer, Ella's gaze shifted to the woman's eyes. It was an odd sight.

One that she hadn't noticed at first... But now, she could notice little else.

GIRL WHO FREEZES SHADOWS

Those eyes glinted the same as Brenner's car keys did, where the keys had caught the faint morning light streaming through the frigid cavern's opening.

Instead of the vibrant gaze one would expect, they were eerily still. It was then that she noticed something peculiar.

"What is it?" Brenner said, noting her reaction.

But she didn't reply right away.

Instead, her gaze narrowed as she stared. "The eyes," she whispered.

"Taxidermy," Brenner reminded her. "Shouldn't be real."

"No... it's... they're not glass."

Indeed, as Ella stared, a cold shiver crept up her spine.

The eyes were not real; they had been meticulously replaced with golden orbs. The metallic sheen seemed to glow faintly against the stark whiteness of the ice.

Brenner moved closer, his brows furrowing in concern. "What do you make of that, Ella?"

Ella's eyes narrowed as she continued to examine the woman's eyes, her mind racing with possibilities. "These eye s... You're right. They're not marbles or glass," she murmured, her voice barely audible amidst the cave's hushed atmosphere. "They're made of gold."

Brenner's eyes widened with surprise. "Gold? That's... what? Gotta be eight ounces, at least?"

"More," Ella said. She hated that she knew it, but growing up in her household, it was hard not to have an eye for the weight of gold.

"Almost twenty thousand dollars," Ella said.

Ella's lips formed a determined line as a realization dawned upon her.

Her face was inches from the ice now, and she could feel the cold chill along her skin.

She murmured, directing her comment towards the forensic tech, "I need the gold analyzed. For sediment, components, anything you can find."

"Sure."

"We need it expedited," Ella added.

"Alright, sure, anything else?"

Brenner's car keys were jangling again, and Ella just gave a brief shake of her head.

"No... No, that's fine. We need to speak with the aunt first. Just... Just call me the moment you hear back on the gold."

And then Ella turned, frowning, feeling a cold shiver down her spine as she began to move hurriedly away, leaving the frozen ballerina with the golden eyes trapped in the cave of ice.

Chapter 5

The dredge mining operation off the coast of Nome was a smaller outfit than Ella was used to in her family's business.

But she watched as the homemade flotation device, complete with sluice box and diver platform, slowly chugged in to harbor, escorted by the coast guard.

She frowned at the approaching dredge, and the single figure clad in a wet suit standing on board.

"Is that the aunt?" Brenner asked at her side.

Ella just nodded once.

The cold wind began to pick up.

With a determined glint in her eyes, Ella stepped onto the weather-beaten docks. The bitter wind whipped through her golden hair, tugging at her coat as if challenging her resolve. Her gaze fixed on a woman in a sleek, black wetsuit, standing atop a dredge miner being guided toward the shore by the vigilant Coast Guard. Little did Addie Harding know her life was about to be shattered by devastating news.

As Ella approached Addie, the salty tang of the sea mingled with the scent of wet wood, permeating her senses. The crash of frigid waves against the hull of the dredge miner filled the air, a rhythmic symphony of nature's power. The early morning sunlight danced on the water's surface, casting shimmering reflections that glinted like shards of glass.

Addie Harding stood with her back straight, surveying the docks with a discerning eye. Her steel-gray eyes revealed a depth of determination, though they held a flicker of something far more severe. Ella approached cautiously, her footsteps muted by the creaking of the docks beneath her. Brenner followed slowly behind, keeping a respectful distance, like a funeral-attendee in pursuit of a pallbearer.

The cold air bit at Ella's skin, seeping through the fabric of her coat. She could feel the chill crawl up her spine, a constant reminder of the frigid Alaskan wilderness that surrounded them. She took a steadying breath, inhaling the crispness of the air as if steeling herself for the conversation that lay ahead.

Ella reached Addie's side just as the Coast Guard completed their careful maneuvering, securing the dredge miner to the dock. The rhythmic thud of the ropes against the wooden pylons seemed to echo the beats of Ella's pounding heart. She cleared her throat, her voice determined yet sympathetic.

"Ms. Harding," Ella began, her tone gentle yet purposeful, "I'm Agent Ella Porter with the FBI. May we speak?"

Addie turned her gaze toward Ella, her eyes narrowing inquisitively. The wind tousled her damp hair, accentuating the fine lines etched on her face, a testament to the resilience she had honed over the years. Sun-bleached skin and age wrinkles marred an otherwise quietly beautiful face. No makeup to speak of and no attempt to conceal a small surgical scar under her chin.

"Agent Porter," Addie acknowledged, her voice carrying the weight of years spent weathering more than one type of storm. "Must be important to bring me off my honey hole."

Ella paused, studying Addie's face, searching for any hint of vulnerability. But Addie's expression remained stoic, a mask of fortitude that concealed any emotion lurking beneath. Did this woman suspect the news? Did she know why she was here?

"I'm here regarding your niece, Lily," Ella replied, her voice barely above a whisper. The words hung in the air, carried away by the biting wind, leaving an eerie silence in their wake.

A flicker of confusion danced across Addie's face before she regained control, her features smoothing into an inscrutable mask. She spoke with practiced composure, her voice void of emotion. "What about Lily?"

Ella's heart sank as she realized Addie was oblivious to the tragedy that had unfolded. She gently reached out, placing a hand on Addie's arm, a gesture of support amidst the brewing storm. The texture of Addie's wet suit was smooth against her fingertips, the neoprene cool beneath her touch.

"Lily..." Ella's voice trembled, her emotions threatening to betray her professionalism. "Lily was found... murdered. I'm so sorry for your loss."

The world seemed to stand still as the weight of Ella's words settled upon Addie's shoulders. The wind whistled mournfully as if grieving alongside the veteran diver. The sea, once a source of tranquility, now roared with a sense of unrelenting sadness.

Addie's eyes widened, the mask of composure slipping for a fraction of a second before she regained control. A tumult of emotions flickered in her gaze, too swift for Ella to decipher. She drew in a deep, shuddering breath, her nostrils flaring with the scent of saltwater mingling with her own raw despair.

Ella watched, her heart heavy, as Addie fought to regain her composure. The wind whipped at their clothes, the chill burrowing deep into their bones. But amidst the frigid surroundings, Ella saw a glimmer of strength in Addie's eyes, a resilience that refused to be extinguished.

"I appreciate you letting me know, Agent Porter," Addie finally replied, her voice steady despite the tremor in her eyes.

Ella nodded, her respect for Addie's fortitude deepening. The salty breeze whispered the sorrow.

"How did it happen?" Addie said after a moment, her expression still one of solemnity.

"It's still under investigation," Ella said, her voice gentle yet firm. "But we'll do everything in our power to find whoever is responsible."

Addie nodded, a tear slipping down her cheek, quickly wiped away. Water droplets spilled from her wet suit onto the dredge deck, and she turned, reaching for the sluice box to remove the mats within. She busied herself unfastening clasps and frowning at the sparse twinkle of a yellow sheen speckled through the coarse sand.

"I suppose you want to know about Lily?" said Addie quietly, her fingers in their gloves, moving at the metal, rusted screws securing the sluice box to the side of the barge.

"Anything you know could help," Ella said, keeping her tone gentle.

The morning sun cast long shadows over the dock as Ella stood near the water's edge, her eyes fixed on the moored gold-mining dredge and its veteran occupant. The rhythmic sound of the waves lapping against the wooden pylons provided a somber backdrop to the task at hand.

When Addie glanced back, holding a mat filled with sediment in one hand, her face was etched with grief, lines of worry creasing her forehead. Her hands trembled slightly as she clutched at the mat, trying to find solace in its weight.

"I don't know if I can help you," she said softly. "How did it all happen? When?"

"We're trying to establish that." The gruesome scene flashed through Ella's mind, but she pushed it aside again. "Addie, I can't imagine the pain you're going through right now," Ella said softly, her voice a reassuring presence. "But we need to find out who did this to Lily. Can you tell me about any friends or acquaintances she had? Anyone who might have wanted to harm her?"

Addie's gaze drifted to the still waters, her voice choked with emotion. "Lily was such a kind soul. She didn't have enemies, as far as I know. She was always so focused on her ballet dreams. That was her entire world."

Ella noted the mention of ballet, a key detail she had been hoping to uncover. The discovery of Lily's body, expertly posed, had sent chills down her spine. However, she decided to withhold this information for now, wanting to gauge Addie's reaction.

"Ballet? Lily was passionate about it?" Ella asked, her tone probing.

A bittersweet smile flickered across Addie's face, her eyes shimmering with pride, catching the flicker of sun off the water. "Yes, ballet was everything to her. She trained for hours every day, pushing herself to the limit. Lily had dreams of becoming a prima ballerina, you know? She was so talented." But Addie shook her head. "We're in Nome, though. There are no ballerinas here. Life doesn't take kindly to the gentler things."

Ella nodded, sharing a quick look with Brenner, whose countenance was somber. "Did Lily ever mention anything strange happening to her? Any encounters or incidents that stood out?"

Addie frowned, her brow knitting together as she recalled past conversations with her niece. "Now that you mention it, there was something. She spoke of a man who used to watch her rehearsals from a distance. Lily said he had a strange energy about him, and it made her uncomfortable. She didn't know who he was, but he always seemed to vanish before she could confront him."

Ella's interest piqued at the mention of the mysterious man. She made a mental note to dig deeper into this potential lead. "Did Lily ever describe this man? Anything distinctive about his appearance?"

Addie shook her head, her eyes clouded with concern. "I'm afraid not. Lily said he wore a hat and kept his face hidden. It's all she could remember. But she was certain that he was watching her. The only reason she mentioned it to me was because he followed her into the parking lot once." Addie bit her lip. "Dear God... I should've paid more attention. I thought it nothing..." A jolt of guilt lanced through Addie's words.

Ella's mind raced with possibilities, connecting the dots between the man Lily had described and the eerie pose of her lifeless body. However, she decided to press on, carefully navigating the conversation.

"Addie, did Lily have any enemies within the ballet community? Rivals who might have wanted to harm her?"

Addie hesitated for a moment, her face reflecting the struggle of her thoughts. "I wouldn't say enemies, but there was one girl, Heather, who always seemed jealous of Lily. She was another aspiring dancer, but her talent didn't quite match Lily's. There was a certain tension between them. Not ballet, mind. Heather was more into classical dances. They have a small hall down by the water. Near the old resin statue."

Ella jotted down the name *Heather*, her mind working through the list of potential suspects. The puzzle was starting to take shape, but there were still missing pieces.

"Addie, thank you for sharing this information. It's crucial in our investigation," Ella said, her voice brimming with sincerity. "Is there anything else you can think of? Even the smallest detail might be significant."

Addie glanced at the gold-mining dredge nearby, her face etched with a mixture of sorrow and determination. "I wish I could help more, Agent Porter. You still haven't told me how she died..."

"I'll update you once we find something," Ella said quickly.

She then turned to Brenner, who was glancing at his phone.

She frowned and mouthed *what* so that Addie couldn't see.

Brenner held up his phone. "They identified the gold."

Ella blinked.

"Gold?" Addie asked.

Ella glanced back. "Was Lily involved in your mining operation?"

"No. No, she hated the water."

Ella felt a shiver at these words, feeling a jolt of sympathy. She'd never been a fan of the ocean. Not for more than a decade.

"Alright. Thank you, ma'am." Ella then turned, and Brenner was already moving.

Ella didn't look back. Couldn't bear too.

She knew so many others like Addie. So many who'd come to Nome, who'd tried to scrape out a living for themselves.

But the cold, harsh climate ate at them.

The thought of Addie's niece... dying alone. It made Ella think of her cousin.

She'd been scheduled to have dinner with Maddie but had been forced to cancel.

Ella pulled her phone from her pocket, and on a whim, sent a quick message. *Hey, Maddie. Dinner?*

Then, she slipped the phone back into her pocket as she reached the parked car with Brenner at her side.

"Coroner's?" he asked.

"Yeah. They identified the gold?"

"Sounds like they found something."

"Then let's hurry."

A cold chill trembled down Ella's spine as the door slammed shut. So far, they'd only found one body.

But with crimes like this... chances were, it was only a matter of time.

And time was the one commodity they didn't have.

Chapter 6

The biting wind cut through Ella's coat as she stepped out of the unmarked FBI vehicle. Her breath formed frosty clouds in the frigid Alaskan air, mingling with the palpable tension that hung over the desolate streets of Nome. It was a town frozen in time, both physically and metaphorically. Ella tightened the collar of her coat, her gloved fingers brushing against the cold metal of her badge as she made her way towards the coroner's office. Inside those walls lay the secrets of Lily's untimely demise, and Ella was determined to uncover them.

The coroner's office loomed ahead, a weathered building surrounded by mounds of snow and ice. Ella pushed open the heavy wooden door, and the warmth of the office washed over her. She was greeted by the familiar scent of disinfectant and a low hum of activity. Her partner, Brenner Gunn, stood near a metal examination table, his tall frame casting a shadow over the room. Dr. Elizabeth Wells, the assistant coroner who was taking over for Dr. Tulip Messer while the coroner was on a big game hunting trip in the mountains.

Dr. Wells was bent over the lifeless body of Lily, her gloved hands moving with precision.

As Ella approached, the room fell silent, and Dr. Wells straightened up, removing her gloves with a practiced motion. Her eyes, tired and pensive, met Ella's, a silent acknowledgment passing between them. Ella had never worked with Dr. Wells before, and her boss, Dr. Messer, was something of a wildcard. Ella wondered if the woman's tendency for eccentricity extended to her hiring process.

"Dr. Wells," Ella began as Brenner came in behind her, his long shadow casting past her.

"You must be Agent Porter," Wells replied, her voice warm.

Dr. Wells boasted a commanding presence. Standing at an average height, she possessed an air of confidence that demanded respect. Her dark brown hair was neatly pulled back into a professional bun, accentuating her sharp facial features. Her piercing hazel eyes seemed to hold a wealth of knowledge, observing every detail with unwavering focus.

The lines on Dr. Wells' face told a story of years spent studying and analyzing the deceased. Fine wrinkles etched the corners of her eyes, hinting at countless hours spent squinting through microscopes and scrutinizing medical reports. Despite the marks of experience, her complexion retained a youthful vitality, a testament to her disciplined lifestyle and dedication to her profession.

She wore a white lab coat that bore evidence of her meticulous work. Stains and faint smudges marked its surface, remnants of the autopsies and investigations she had conducted. Beneath the coat she wore a professional attire, choosing tailored blouses and trousers that conveyed both authority and practicality.

Dr. Wells' hands, though delicate, were calloused from years of meticulous work.

Ella nodded in greeting. Brenner hung back, lounging against the doorway, his arms crossed.

Ella's eyes moved to the lone figure on the gurney behind the coroner.

She stared at the pale skin, the stiff corpse.

"Still frozen?" Ella asked.

"Thawed some," replied the coroner. She frowned.

Ella wanted to but kept her expression a mask. It seemed... unkind... to refer to the body as one might discuss a slab of meat.

She interjected quickly. "What can you tell us about the cause of death?"

Dr. Wells sighed, her breath visible in the chilled room. "It's a baffling case, Agent Porter," she replied, her voice tinged with weariness. "Lily's body was found in a rather peculiar state. She froze to death."

Ella's brows furrowed in confusion. "So she was frozen in the caves?"

"No. No, she was frozen before the body was moved. Frozen in the pose you saw when you discovered her."

The coroner motioned towards the examination table, where Lily's lifeless form lay. Ella moved closer, her eyes scanning every detail. Lily's limbs were contorted in an unnatural position, her delicate features locked in an eternal expression of agony. Ice crystals clung to her skin, shimmering in the harsh fluorescent light.

"Whoever did this wanted to preserve her, almost like a taxidermy animal," Dr. Wells explained, her voice filled with a mix of revulsion and fascination. "But that's not the most disturbing part. Look at her eyes."

Ella's gaze shifted to Lily's face, and she spotted where the golden orbs stared back at her. It was as if Lily's vacant gaze held a hidden message, a secret that begged to be deciphered.

"The eyes are filled with gold," Ella said, her voice barely audible. "I spotted it back in the caves. I was told you had a mineral deposit report."

Dr. Wells nodded, her voice hushed. "It's not just any gold. There's something peculiar about it. We found traces of black sand mixed in. It suggests that the gold wasn't pure and hadn't been processed well. It's an unusual combination."

"How unusual? What percentage were the trace minerals?"

"The gold was only about eighty-five percent pure, all said and done. I found some pyrite mixed in."

"Fool's gold?" Brenner called from the doorway. "That's not usual, is it? I didn't even know we had pyrite sucked up by those dredges."

Ella was shaking her head. "We don't. Someone is cutting the gold?"

"Cutting it how?"

She looked back at where Brenner's handsome features had creased into a frown. She said, "Cutting it by adding the minerals after. Probably selling it at a higher-purity claim. Sort of like mixing coke with baby powder."

Brenner sniffed. "Can't be a reputable processing plant."

"No, but Nome is filled with all sorts of clean-up plants," Ella said with a shrug. She paused, though, hesitating. "But pyrite... *and* black sand?" Her brow wrinkled.

Ella's mind raced, connecting the dots. The gold, the processing plant, and the macabre display of Lily's body. It was all starting to form a chilling picture in her mind. There was a method to the madness, a twisted logic that guided the killer's hand.

Brenner, who had been silent until now, spoke up. "So we have a killer who freezes their victims and stuffs them like trophies. But why the gold? What's the significance?"

Dr. Wells sighed, her voice heavy with uncertainty. "That, my friends, is the million-dollar question. Even in its impure state, it's worth... Nearly fifteen thousand dollars."

Ella gave a low whistle.

Brenner crossed his arms, shaking his head. "I mean... maybe we can ask around," he said. "Find if anyone knows someone who's been cutting their gold."

"Or," Ella said quietly, biting her lip as she did, "We can go to the source."

"How's that?"

"A source, I should say. Someone who knows all the wash plants in Nome. Someone whose job it is to keep track of the competition."

Dr. Wells was watching them both while wearing an expression of curiosity. Brenner on the other hand had gone still and was frowning. He shook his head. "No."

Ella turned to face him. "I don't want to either."

"No," he repeated, more firmly.

"They know everyone. They know everyone connected."

Brenner scowled.

"Besides," Ella said, "she owes you one."

"NO!"

"She does! You saved her life."

Brenner frowned, his blue eyes glinting like chips of ice as he glared at her.

But Ella turned away, already shaking her head and muttering to herself.

"Yes... yes..." she was saying. "We have to." She said it under her breath, speaking firmly, realizing she was trying to convince herself.

As much as her family hated her, and as much as her twin sister went out of her way to cause trouble, Ella was aware that no one knew gold nearly as well in all of Nome.

She loosed a long sigh, giving a quick nod to the coroner. "Can you email me a copy of the file when you get a chance?"

And then she turned, moving towards the exit, already plotting the course in her mind which would take her to her sister's home.

Chapter 7

Ella and Brenner both sat in the driveway, their breath fogging the inside of the glass as they stared up at the large mansion which belonged to Priscilla Porter and Chief Matthias Baker. The couple known by many as the sweethearts of Nome.

Neither of them wanted to get out of the car. Ella hadn't even unbuckled. She just sat there, cold, staring at the house, and gnawing at her lip.

"Maybe this isn't such a good idea," Ella murmured.

Brenner just grunted. "That's what I've been saying."

"Maybe..." Ella sighed, closed her eyes, then summoned her courage, pushing out of the car onto the asphalt and turning to acknowledge the large mansion.

The home looked like something out of a fairytale, with its white columns and ornate balconies. Brenner had grown up in a modest trailer on the outskirts of town, and the ostentatious display of wealth made him uncomfortable. Ella could tell in the way he shifted his posture and rubbed at his knuckles, his gaze glancing off in every direction.

Still, Brenner was following her lead, his expression wary. "Let's just get this over with," he said, noting her attention.

She forced a quick nod.

They walked up the path, the crunching of gravel beneath their boots echoing in the tranquil silence. As they reached the front door, Ella hesitated, her hand hovering over the brass knocker.

"What are we going to say?" she asked Brenner, her voice shaking.

"I don't know. This was your idea."

"Right. The truth. Priscilla likes the truth."

"Priscilla likes hurting feelings. The truth just sometimes helps with that."

"Well... We tell her we're investigating a murder case and ask if she knows anything about the processing plants. Simple as that."

Ella took a deep breath and knocked on the door. She heard footsteps approaching and quickly stepped back, standing next to Brenner.

The door opened to reveal a middle-aged woman with graying hair, wearing a crisp white blouse and a pencil skirt. Her eyes widened in surprise as she recognized Brenner.

"Ma'am," Brenner said, his voice respectful. "I'm sorry to disturb you, but we need to speak with Ms. Porter."

"Of course," the woman said after a moment of hesitation, her eyes sliding to Ella, then back to Brenner. She stepped back to let them in. "Please, follow me."

As they walked through the opulent halls, Ella couldn't help but feel like an intruder. The air was heavy with the scent of rich perfume, and the walls were adorned with expensive paintings and intricate tapestries.

Finally, they reached the living room.

Ella paused, staring within. A figure was hunched over a desk, sitting in a tall, leatherbound chair. The figure in question had the same blond hair as Ella. The same pretty, tired features. Her hair was pulled back in a pony-tail, and her ears were pierced, displaying seashell earrings.

Priscilla was murmuring to herself as she tapped away on a keyboard, the glow of the computer screen illuminating her features.

Ella's heart sank as she saw her sister. There was a time when they were close. When they shared secrets and made each other laugh. But those days were long gone.

"Priscilla," Ella said, her voice soft yet firm.

Priscilla turned around, squinting at them for a moment before recognition flashed in her eyes. Her expression seemed to harden. Priscilla rolled her eyes, emphatically, making no effort to conceal her reaction at the site of her sister. "Ella," she said, sighing. "Why are you here?"

"We're investigating a murder," Brenner said curtly, stepping forward. "And we need to know if you have any information about gold processing plants. Clean up shops outside the usual grid of things."

Priscilla blinked, turning fully now. She was wearing a white blouse, and her arms crossed slowly over it. Perhaps it was Ella's imagination, but it almost seemed as if Cilla was attempting to accentuate her chest towards Brenner.

"Straight and to the point, then?" she said in a falsely sweet voice. "No hello? No 'I miss you, dearie'? We did have a child together, after all, Brenner." She then held a hand to her lips. "Oops. Sorry. You did know that, didn't you, Ella?"

Brenner scowled.

Ella just sighed. "Do we have to? Really?"

"Have to what?" the same treacle sweet voice.

Ella just shook her head. "We need to ask about wash plants."

Priscilla's face twisted with disgust. "Wash plants? Do I look like someone who would know anything about some small-timer's clean-up crew?"

"You know everyone in Nome," Ella said, feeling a spark of anger. But she hid the feeling.

Priscilla, on the other hand, had no such aversion to withholding emotion. She rolled her eyes emphatically a second time. "Typical. Always trying to play the hero, aren't you, Ella?

Well, I don't know anything. And even if I did, why would I tell you?"

Brenner stepped in, his voice low. "You owe me."

Priscilla considered him for a moment, then let out a sarcastic laugh. "Owe you? That's the play, then?"

"I saved your life."

Priscilla looked ready to retort again, but she ran her tongue along her lower lip, then released a soft sigh. "Alright, then," she murmured. "If that's how you want it to be."

"We just need your help, Cilla," Ella murmured, trying to keep her tone even.

Brenner looked away, staring out the window. And while he wasn't looking, Priscilla seemed to study his silhouette.

Priscilla's expression softened, just a bit, but when she caught her sister looking, her eyes hardened again.

"What exactly are you looking for?" Priscilla was sorting papers on her desk now, moving them around, though it seemed as if she were simply trying to find something to do with her hands.

"A bad clean-up," Ella said. "Alloy. Black sand. And mixed in pyrite."

"Fool's gold?"

Priscilla's eyebrow quirked. And for a moment, she looked more curious than irritated.

Ella went quiet, knowing her sister well enough to allow the loose thread to loose her lips.

"I mean... there's only one outfit dumb enough to try something like that. They operate out of an old junkyard."

"Which yard?"

"Just called *Nome Assembly.*"

"Who owns it?" Ella asked.

Priscilla shrugged, still arranging her papers. "I don't know. They're careful, but they have a reputation for being greedy idiots."

Brenner stepped forward. "And you don't know their name?"

"I don't get involved with the small-time stuff," Priscilla said, her voice hardening again. "Look, I've given you what I can. We're done here."

Ella nodded, feeling a sense of disappointment. She knew that getting information from her sister was like trying to get blood from a stone. But it still stung knowing that even after all these years, Priscilla was still so closed off to her.

Ella paused, watching as her sister turned towards a safe in the wall.

"Just... be careful, alright, Priscilla?" Ella said.

Her sister tensed, her shoulders going still. She remained facing the wall. "Is that a threat?"

"No. No, of course not. It's a plea."

But Cilla didn't turn around again. Ella shared a look with Brenner, who looked like he wanted nothing more than to flee. With a sigh and a shrug, Ella turned.

She knew Cilla well enough to know when a stay was past its welcome.

She began moving back down the hall, frowning as she did.

Brenner fell into step at her side. In the hall, he murmured, loud enough so only she could hear, "Well, that went well."

Ella didn't respond to the sarcasm. Instead, she said, "We should check out the junkyard."

"You really think these gold washers are involved? Seems kinda outside their MO."

"Their gold ended up in our victim's eyes somehow. Just gotta follow the evidence. Wherever it leads." Tight-lipped, she stepped out of her sister's home, back onto the patio.

As she did, it was as if a weight left her shoulders.

And she began moving hurriedly down the steps, towards the waiting car.

Chapter 8

The frozen wind whistled through the desolate junkyard, where remnants of broken dreams lay strewn across the barren landscape. Ella and Brenner parked their unmarked, black sedan near the rusty gate that guarded the entrance to the shady business.

Ella shifted uncomfortably as she pushed open the door, and a gust of chill wind swept through the vehicle, tugging at her jacket sleeves. She scanned the area, noting the eerie silence that hung in the air like a heavy shroud.

The junkyard had tall, rusted, barbed wire fences encircling it. Through the gaps in the fence, Ella spotted a maze of rust and metal. Piles of scrap metal glinted in the sunlight, casting a metallic sheen across the yard.

Brenner led the way, his footsteps crunching on the gravel as he made his way towards the entrance. Ella followed closely behind, her hand poised near her hidden weapon.

As they approached the gate, a burly man with a permanent scowl emerged from a makeshift booth, his hands casually resting on his hips. His gaze locked onto the agents, distrust oozing from every pore of his weathered face. He raised a meaty hand, halting their progress.

"Sorry, folks," the gatekeeper grumbled, his voice gravelly. "This place ain't open to the public."

Ella flashed her badge, her steel-blue eyes glinting with determination. "FBI. Are you the owner?"

The gatekeeper's expression tightened, his mistrust deepening. "Look, lady, I don't care who you are. The boss said no one's allowed in."

Brenner stepped forward, his towering frame casting a long shadow over the gatekeeper. "Listen, pal, we don't have time for games. Let us in, or we'll find a way in ourselves."

The gatekeeper's eyes narrowed, his resolve hardening. "You can try, tough guy, but it won't end well for you."

Brenner tensed, but Ella's hand shot out, catching his arm and giving a gentle tug.

He glanced at her, sighed, and the two of them retreated a few paces, exchanging a knowing glance. They stepped away from the gate, concealing themselves behind a dilapidated storage shed.

Brenner nodded towards the guard, keeping his voice low. "I've seen him around before. Rough guy. No brains. No diving ability. Just the muscle."

She nodded, standing in the shadow of the shed, which pressed against the back of the metal fence.

The guard's shadow was shifting, as if he were trying to move to get a good look at them.

But she ignored this. "I need a distraction," she said.

"I could just arrest him."

"No. No, we don't want to kick over a nest until we know what's in it."

Brenner frowned. "I can chat with him a bit. If you wanna..." He made a shooing motion.

She paused briefly, under the sun. Her mind wandered back to the corpse in the ice caves. The ballerina frozen in a frigid dance.

She sighed then nodded.

Brenner began to move once more, raising a hand as he emerged, gesturing at the guard.

As he called out, his voice ringing, Ella also moved. With a calculated nod, she slipped away, her footsteps soft against the frozen ground.

She moved around behind the shed. It created a sort of barricade, concealing her from the view of the guard at the gate.

Keeping the shed between her and the guard, she began to tug at sections of the rusted fence, looking for loose purchase.

Now, she could hear Brenner chatting with the guard. The two men like a couple of alpha wolves sniffing at each other, sizing the other up.

She hoped Brenner didn't do any *permanent* damage to the guard.

Her fingers pried through the gaps in the fence, caught, then tugged hard.

The fence rattled, and dust tumbled. Then, she found some give. She yanked some more, and the fence came away, revealing a sort of metal flap towards the base of the barricade.

She felt a thrill of exhilaration.

Then, still listening to the hum of voices beyond the shed, she ducked and slipped through the gap under the fence, her shadow melding with that of the shed.

Ella crouched down, looking around for any signs of danger. The shadows grew longer, and the cold air seemed more biting. She quickened her pace, moving stealthily through the maze of scrap metal and rubble, her eyes scanning for anything untoward. She was looking for a gold clean-up shed hidden in all this.

And one thing was certain about the denizens of Nome.

Anyone intruding on a gold shed would be met with deadly force.

GIRL WHO FREEZES SHADOWS

The scent of oil and rust hung heavy in the air as she weaved between abandoned vehicles, her senses sharpened by the anticipation of the unknown.

Behind her, in the distance, Brenner engaged the gatekeeper in a heated argument, his commanding presence creating a diversion. The guard's attention firmly fixed on her partner, Ella seized the opportunity and slipped behind a row of towering earth-moving machines.

The junkyard was a labyrinth of forgotten treasures and discarded memories. Ella's heart pounded in her chest as she maneuvered through the rusted remains. Her fingers grazed over the rough surfaces of wrecked cars, her breath visible in the frigid air.

But her stealthy advance was short-lived. As she rounded a corner, turning towards a large warehouse-shaped structure in the center of it all, she froze.

Three sets of eyes blinked back at her.

She swallowed.

The eyes blinked again.

"Shit," she whispered under her breath.

But the sound of the expletive was nearly lost to the guttural growling of the beasts.

She found herself face-to-face with three snarling pitbulls, their muscular bodies poised to strike.

They weren't chained to anything, either.

Ella's heart skipped a beat as her instincts kicked into over-drive.

The dogs had temporarily paused as if confused why a slab of meat had just *wandered* towards them.

But now, they were quickly getting over their initial surprise.

They snarled and lunged.

Ella yelped, spinning on her heel.

She took two lunging steps towards an abandoned pickup truck, planted one hand on the hood, the grainy metal rough against her fingers, and then vaulted on top of the truck.

Without hesitation, she sprinted across the roof, her boots clanging against the corroded metal. The pitbulls pursued, their barks echoing through the desolate junkyard. Ella's mind raced, adrenaline surging through her veins.

She leaped from one precarious perch to another, balancing on the edges of rusted roofs and abandoned digging machines. The pitbulls below snarled and snapped, their teeth mere inches from her heels. Each stride she took brought her closer to the warehouse.

Finally, with her heart pounding in her ears, Ella spotted a semi-truck, its cab pointed to a rickety catwalk circling the second level of the warehouse.

GIRL WHO FREEZES SHADOWS

The dogs were still braying, the sounds of their paws in rapid pursuit. She pushed herself to her limits, her muscles screaming in protest as she propelled herself upward. The pitbulls' fervent pursuit continued, their barks reverberating off the walls of the junkyard.

With one final burst of energy, arms straining, Ella clambered over the wheel hub and hood of the parked semi and reached the safety of the catwalk, her breath coming in ragged gasps. She looked down at the pitbulls, their fierce eyes still fixed on her, their barks reduced to a distant echo.

She breathed heavily, sweat prickling along her forehead.

Ella took a moment to collect herself, the intensity of the chase still coursing through her veins.

Far behind her, Brenner continued to engage the gatekeeper, their voices growing fainter as Ella pressed against the corrugated warehouse wall, moving along the creaking walkway, approaching the metal door.

She pressed a shoulder against the door, and that's when she heard new voices.

Rough, cold tones. A snapping, authoritative voice.

Shivers trembled down her spine.

Ella pressed her ear against the door and strained to hear more. The voices grew louder, and she recognized the sound of men arguing. They spoke in low, hushed tones, but their words were clear enough to make out.

"Where's the shipment?" one man growled.

"It's on its way," another voice replied. "But it'll be late."

"I don't want excuses. I want results."

Ella's heart raced.

She took a deep breath and pushed open the door slowly, inching it open with her shoulder. It groaned on its rusty hinges, and she grimaced at the sound, moving slowly. Once the door propped open, a bright, white fluorescent light extended from inside the warehouse, bathing her along the walkway.

She stepped into the brightly lit warehouse, still crouched, her eyes adjusting to the sudden, faux-light source. She could see crates and boxes stacked high along the walls, and several men standing in a huddle near the back of the room.

They were standing near powder-gold recovery equipment. One, large, rotating circular item trickled with a steady flow of water, showing flashes of gold from ridges along its center.

Another trough was being shoveled as a man tried to dislodge sediment into a painter's bucket.

She counted six men in total. Three of them were heavily armed.

Ella crouched on the top floor of the brightly lit warehouse, her heart pounding with anticipation. She carefully peered over the railing, her eyes fixed on the armed men below who were meticulously cleaning gold. The air was thick with the metallic scent.

Ella surveyed the dilapidated warehouse. She could see from her vantage point that it had been divided and converted into a makeshift gold wash plant, stocked with machines and supplies used to separate usable gold from sediment.

She moved along the walkway, keeping to the shadows cast by the rail, approaching the metal steps in the back of the warehouse.

She took the steps slowly, moving quietly, inching forward.

As she observed the men below, her attention was drawn to a figure off to the side. He stood out from the rest, exuding an air of elegance that seemed out of place in this grungy environment. He wore a neat suit and shining shoes. The boss?

Someone else?

Swiftly, she took out her smartphone, expertly capturing a discreet photo of the man. She quickly ran a search on her phone, comparing the image to known criminal records.

She tensed, halfway down the stairs, still crouched, still hidden, watching the database loading bar whir on her phone.

"Come on," she whispered in a nearly inaudible voice.

And then, the AI-generated facial recognition returned a result.

Bradley Martyn.

She clicked the link and frowned. Multiple assault charges against women. Released on bail two months ago. Right before the murder.

Ella's focus sharpened, and she returned her attention to the well-dressed man with the polished shoes.

He was addressing one of the thugs cleaning the gold. But then, he nodded and turned.

Ella watched as the man made his way towards a dark hall in the back of the warehouse. Seizing the chance, she quietly slipped away from her vantage point, hugging the shadows as she trailed down the stairs and moved along the wall, heading towards the safe hall. He paused briefly, and she froze, behind two, large crates, sucking in her gut and going very still.

The man's eyes seemed to scan the shadows, but then, he scratched at his chin, shook his head, and disappeared into the hall.

She took a breath, waited, then followed.

The warehouse's layout was labyrinthine, a maze of hallways and dark corners. Ella's footsteps were nearly silent as she weaved through the corridors, her senses heightened, and her training guiding her every move. She kept far back enough that she wouldn't be noticed. But ahead, she kept an eye on the retreating form of Mr. Martyn.

Finally, the man reached a heavy, creaking door at the end of a dimly lit hallway. He disappeared into the darkness beyond, and Ella's curiosity overpowered her caution. Determined not to lose sight of him, she crept forward, inch by inch, her heart pounding in her chest.

As she descended into the basement, the air grew colder and thicker, a sharp contrast to the hustle and bustle of the warehouse above. A faint flicker of light emanated from somewhere ahead, casting eerie shadows on the damp, concrete walls. The sound of dripping water echoed through the narrow space, intensifying the sense of unease.

Ella pressed on, her senses heightened as she drew closer to the source of the light. Suddenly, she found herself in a small chamber, illuminated by a single dim bulb hanging from the ceiling. The room was cluttered with discarded crates and rusty equipment, creating a haunting atmosphere.

Her eyes scanned the room, and her heart skipped a beat when she spotted the man. He stood hunched over a table, inspecting a collection of peculiar objects. Ella strained to make out the details, her mind racing to connect the dots.

Then, she saw it. The fool's gold and pyrite she had encountered earlier on the top floor were now arranged in a makeshift display.

Focusing her attention back on the man, Ella observed him meticulously examining one particular ounce tube—a golden container.

With steady hands, she discreetly snapped more photos, capturing the incriminating scene.

Just as she was about to retreat, a stray beam of light caught her eye. It glinted off something obscured beneath a dusty sheet. She stood about twenty paces behind Mr. Martyn, and for the moment, he hadn't spotted her. Intrigued, Ella cautiously approached the covered object, her curiosity overpowering the danger that lurked around her.

She reached out and pulled back the sheet, revealing a locked chest. It was weathered and worn, bearing the scars of time.

There was water damage along the chest, as well as barnacles encrusting one side. Had it been recovered during a mining operation?

She frowned, staring at the chest.

Her fingers pried at soft, soggy wood, but to no avail. The thing was locked shut. She moved her fingers along the grooves and found an opening in the back where the wood had cracked. Her fingers came away caked in what looked like white flour.

She paused, stared. And then her eyes widened.

Cocaine.

A jolt through her chest. Not just a mining operation, then. But an illicit drug trade. Drug dealers were often far less reasonable than gold miners—the sort of unreasonable that often ended with a bullet.

She wiped her hand off on the moldered wood.

GIRL WHO FREEZES SHADOWS

Ella peered cautiously through the dark hallway, her breath steady and her senses on high alert. The flickering light from a dying bulb cast eerie shadows on the peeling wallpaper of the abandoned building. A musty smell filled her nostrils, the scent of rot and decay intermingling with the faint trace of burned rubber, a remnant from an evident fire that had claimed the far, charred wall, years ago. She swallowed hard.

Ella's fingers tightened around the grip of her firearm as she advanced further into the gloom. The darkness seemed to close in around her, but she refused to let it deter her. She had trained for situations like this, endless hours spent honing her instincts.

"Come on, you bastard," she muttered under her breath, her voice a low growl. "Show yourself."

She shook her head in frustration, turning away from the chest and glancing back towards...

She froze.

He was gone.

She frowned.

Missing—where was he?

And then she heard the faintest of motions. A scrape of a foot against the cold ground.

She turned sharply, just in time to avoid the knife slicing towards her throat.

Chapter 9

Ella dodged the first knife attack from the unseen assailant, feeling the cold metal whistle by, scraping along her neck. She stumbled back with a desperate gasp, one hand flung out to strike at the attacker's wrist. The assailant snarled, wreathed in shadows, avoiding her blow; he lunged forward, his blade glinting in the moonlight as he slashed at Ella with a fierce, sweeping motion. Ella just barely managed to dodge the attack, feeling the wind from the blade rush by her face.

There was no time to recover. Only time for instinct. With a fierce cry, Ella sprang into action, launching a series of lightning-fast strikes towards her attacker, deciding that offense would give her some space to think.

One of her blows caught his neck. The other grazed his shoulder as he dodged. As she pushed towards him, knocking him under the flickering bulb above, she glimpsed his features. In a brief snapshot of an instant, a figure emerged from the shadows, materializing into view like a sinister apparition. The man was tall and gaunt, his features obscured by the shadows cast by the flickering bulb. In his hand, he wielded a wicked-looking knife that glinted menacingly in the dim light.

"I see you," Ella whispered, her adrenaline beginning to surge through her veins.

There was a momentary lull to their deadly dance. Both of them sizing the other up.

The man didn't have the shoes or hands of a laborer. Maybe a lawyer, or a banker. But he wielded the knife with no small amount of experience.

The two of them swayed in the shadows, facing each other, half-crouched as if preparing to spring into action like some fierce predators. In that lull, she studied the man's movements carefully, noting the way he shifted his weight from one foot to the other, the subtle flexing of his fingers around the knife's handle. He was clearly nervous, but also dangerous—a volatile combination.

"Drop the knife!" Ella commanded, her fingers tensed. She didn't move for her gun yet.

She knew the moment she did, he'd close the distance. A knife fighter could cover ten yards in a split second. The man didn't respond verbally, but the soft chuckle that escaped his lips sent a chill down Ella's spine. He took a step toward her, the knife held high above his head, ready to strike.

"Last chance," Ella warned, her voice steady despite the pounding of her heart. But the man continued to advance, his movements slow and deliberate like a predator stalking its prey.

She went for her gun.

He lunged at her.

Her years of FBI training kicked in as she changed tactics last moment. Instead of pulling her firearm, which would've been useless in such close quarters, she lifted her hand from her gun and went for the attacker, grabbing his wrist with a vice-like grip and twisting. The suddenness of her attack seemed to catch him off guard, and he let out an involuntary grunt of surprise.

Ella hissed through gritted teeth as she yanked his arm downward, using his own momentum against him. She could see the shock register on his face as he realized he wasn't facing a random person in the dark. She had training, years of it. And she moved fast.

With her free hand, Ella swiftly grabbed the back of his neck, pulling him closer as she simultaneously pivoted on one foot and slid her leg behind his knees. The next step in the judo throw was critical, and she executed it flawlessly, applying pressure upward on the attacker's arm and downward on his neck.

"Ugh!" the man gasped as he found himself suddenly airborne, his feet no longer in contact with the cold, damp floor of the hallway. For a split second, time seemed to slow down, and Ella felt a grim satisfaction as she saw the dawning realization in his eyes that he had severely underestimated her.

With a sickening crunch, the man slammed into the ground, the impact reverberating throughout the narrow space. The knife clattered to the floor, skidding away from his limp fingers. Ella didn't waste any time; she quickly snatched it up, tossing it out of his reach.

She spat, breathing heavily as she stood over him. The man groaned in pain, his body writhing as he tried to break free from her hold.

"Go to hell," he managed to choke out, his voice thick with pain and anger.

Ella didn't reply. She wasn't the sort to taunt an assailant. One moment, she'd been poised, laced with adrenaline, moving fast. The next, reserved and calm again. Attentive and watchful, it was like a magical transformation.

Ella's shoulders slumped as she let out a shuddering breath, the adrenaline that had sustained her through the fight beginning to ebb. Her chest heaved with exertion, and sweat trickled down her spine, making her shiver in the dankness of the hallway. For a moment, she allowed herself to savor the victory, closing her eyes and taking in the musty scent of the air around her.

The assailant remained on the ground, groaning. She tugged at his wrists, and all fight seemed to have left him as she secured the handcuffs, locking them tightly into place.

But just then, she paused, frowning.

The man's eyes widened, clearly having heard the sound as well. He opened his mouth to call out, but she clapped a hand over his lips, grimacing at the warm, damp breath against her palm.

Instead, she listened, her spine prickling as fear coursed through her.

Her ears pricked up at the sound of footsteps approaching, echoing ominously in the darkness. She tensed, every muscle in her body coiling like a spring, ready for whatever new threat might be coming her way.

"Dammit," she muttered quietly, trying and failing to keep the edge of weariness from her voice. The footsteps faltered, then resumed, growing louder and more insistent.

Two figures emerged from the shadows, their faces obscured by the dim light. They were tall and broad-shouldered, dressed in dark workman clothing stained in grease that seemed to swallow what little illumination was available. Ella's heart skipped a beat as she saw the glint of metal in their hands—one carried a baseball bat, the other a crowbar. Their steps were heavy and deliberate as they approached. The two men were frowning, glancing back and forth, their gaze scanning the dark corners.

"I swear I heard something," one was saying.

And then he went quiet. The two men both stared directly at Ella.

Her heart skipped a beat.

It took the men a second to glance from her to the man on the ground.

"Looks like we've got ourselves a hero," the one with the baseball bat sneered, his words dripping with disdain.

"More like a dead hero," the other retorted, brandishing his crowbar like a weapon. They moved in unison, flanking Ella on either side as if they had rehearsed the maneuver a dozen times before.

Ella's mind raced, trying to calculate her odds of success against two armed attackers. She was tired, her limbs heavy with fatigue, but she wasn't ready to go down without a fight. Her hand moved to her holster, tightening its grip on her weapon.

"Listen," she said, forcing a confidence she didn't truly feel into her voice. "You don't want to do this. I'm not here about the drugs."

"An' if we do wanna?" the one with the crowbar challenged, his tone mocking.

Ella's gaze darted between the two men, her heart pounding in her ears. She knew she couldn't take them both on without her gunshots alerting the entire junkyard, including multiple armed assailants, but maybe she didn't have to. Swallowing her fear, she lunged toward the unconscious man on the floor, wrenching his arm behind his back and positioning him in front of her as a human shield. The cold metal of her handgun pressed against his temple.

"Stop!" she commanded, her voice steady despite the thunderous pulse in her veins. "One step closer, and I pull the trigger."

It was a gambit. She was assuming the man was some sort of head honcho. And now, their reactions would tell the story.

The attackers hesitated, their weapons lowered just slightly. In that moment of uncertainty, her instincts took over. A single gunshot... a risk, but maybe a necessary one. She timed the bullet with the distant sound of clanking machinery from the clean-up room, masking it as best she could. Ella fired a warning shot into the ceiling, the *crack* echoing through the hallway, but swallowed by the machine sounds. Dust rained down from the bullet hole, causing the men to flinch and shield their eyes.

"Next one goes in his head," Ella threatened, her words ice-cold, though she didn't feel it. Had anyone heard the gunshot? Would more shooters come to investigate? It was all instinct now. She had to trust something. She put more venom into her voice, "And after that? You're next."

The man with the baseball bat shifted his weight from foot to foot, his grip tightening around the weapon. "You think you can shoot both of us before we get to you?" he asked, his voice wavering ever so slightly.

"Want to find out?" Ella countered, locking eyes with him. She could feel the sweat trickling down her spine, but she refused to let her nerves show. There was no room for weakness here – not if she wanted to make it out alive.

"Look, lady," the other attacker began, his crowbar still raised, but his stance less aggressive now. "We don't want any trouble. We were just—"

"Save it," Ella snapped, cutting him off. "I don't care what you were 'just' doing. Right now, what you're going to do is drop your weapons and back away."

The two men exchanged a glance, their hesitation evident in the uneasy silence that followed. As seconds ticked by, Ella's grip on the unconscious man tightened, her muscles coiled like a spring, ready to unleash hell if needed.

"Drop them," she repeated, her voice cold and unyielding.

Finally, with a curse, the man with the crowbar let it clatter to the floor. The baseball bat soon followed suit, the noise of its impact echoing through the dark hallway. With their weapons relinquished, the two attackers raised their hands in surrender, their bravado gone, replaced by a newfound wariness.

But Ella wasn't here to bust a drug ring. She was after a murderer. The gold that had been found in the victim's eyes had been processed *here*. She needed more information.

Now, ears peeled for even the slightest sound of approaching steps, she returned her full attention to her temporary captives.

"Sit down," Ella ordered the two surrendering attackers, gesturing with her gun toward the floor. They complied without hesitation, their expressions a mixture of fear and frustration, their eyes glancing towards the man in cuffs. Clearly, he had clout.

The stench of sweat and fear hung heavy in the air, mingling with the acrid tang of gunpowder residue. The faint buzz of a flickering light overhead joined the labored breathing of the surrendered men on the ground, creating an eerie soundtrack to the standoff.

The man in cuffs, in the yuppie shoes, was trying to move.

"Stay where you are," Ella commanded, her voice firm but laced with the ragged edge of fatigue. Her heart pounded in her chest like a trapped bird, adrenaline coursing through her veins as she tried to make sense of the situation.

The man had turned his gaunt features to look up at her. A single tear drop tattoo traced the outside of his left eye.

He glared at her, his expression more petulant than unnerving.

"Don't move!" she commanded again.

"Of course," the man said, raising his cuffed hands in mock surrender. His voice was smooth and cultured, a stark contrast to the gruff snarls of the previous attackers. "I wouldn't dream of getting in your way, agent..." His cultured words didn't quite match his twisted features.

As he spoke, Ella's mind raced—desperately scanning the dark hallway for any signs of danger or potential escape routes. The high-pitched creak of a door hinge caught her attention, followed by the distant echo of footsteps. She knew backup would be arriving soon, but every second that ticked by felt like an eternity.

"Who are you?" she demanded, trying to maintain control over the conversation. Her muscles tensed with anticipation, ready to spring into action at the slightest hint of aggression from the man.

She already had his name and face. Still had it logged on her phone—more importantly, she knew his record against women.

"I'm just an interested party," he replied nonchalantly, his eyes never leaving hers. He managed to control his expression now, communicating confidence that hadn't been there before. He said, "And who are you?"

"That's not important, Mr. Martyn. Now stop moving towards me," she warned, her grip on the gun tightening ever so slightly.

The man's smile faded, replaced by a calculated expression that made Ella's skin crawl. "Very well," he said, his voice dropping to a conspiratorial whisper. He went still, where previously he'd been inching along the ground in her direction. "This place isn't what it looks like. Do you even have a warrant?"

She cast her gaze towards the two thugs in workman clothes, facing the ground. They remained obediently still.

She returned her attention to the creep.

"You dilute gold with sediment and pyrite," she said simply. "I don't care about the drugs."

"You called me Mr. Martyn," he said. "You know me?"

A flicker of fear across his expression.

"I've done my research," she said. "So has my team." She didn't outright say it, but she wanted him to think the whole place was surrounded.

She could see his concern now, etched across every line in his face.

He stared at her, tense, his lips pressed tightly together. The cuffs glinted dully from the flickering bulb above as he shifted his weight at her feet.

"What's got you so interested in our gold?" he said. "Ain't a crime to have a bad clean up."

"Unless you advertise as pure."

"Whatever," he snapped.

"I saw the Royal Water vats," she said. "You *can* separate the gold. You just choose not to."

"The acid? So you know your alloys."

She just shook her head, not wanting to get into a discussion on the finer points of separating chunk gold from sediment. Instead, she said, "Where were you last night?"

"Excuse me?"

"You heard me."

GIRL WHO FREEZES SHADOWS

He stared at her. "Last night? Here. And I can prove it."

She frowned. "How?"

"Security cameras," he shot back, jutting out his chin.

Her eyes darted past the two prone men, again looking towards the far hall. But the sounds she'd heard earlier had faded.

But time was still ticking.

She said, "Show me."

"Can't. Cuffed."

"Your hands are in front. Pull your phone, and show me," she snapped.

He glared at her, but when she didn't flinch, he reluctantly, with some difficulty and much jangling of chains, reached into his pocket and procured a phone.

"Take a look," he said, flipping through the camera roll. "There's my alibi."

Ella took the phone from him, scanning through the footage. It was blurry and grainy, but she could see enough to verify that he was, indeed, in the building the previous night, unmistakable in the footage near the gold clean up. In one scene, she spotted him berating one of the men who was currently laying on the floor.

She let out a faint sigh, briefly massaging the bridge of her nose.

And that's when she heard the sound of sirens. She glanced at the phone again, cursing.

The siren continued to wail. She paused, thinking for a second, and then she pocketed the phone.

"Hey! That's mine!"

She didn't reply. Instead, she turned on her heel and broke into a dead sprint, racing away.

The only lead was the gold. Which meant that the phone belonging to the man who *sold* the gold would be more useful than the man himself.

Phones didn't lie.

Criminals did.

She heard voices behind her. The siren continued to wail, and her footsteps pounded the pavement in the dark hallway as she raced to the exit. She would need to find Brenner and get out, *fast*.

Chapter 10

Brenner was waiting for Ella as she hastened back to the car, stolen phone clutched in hand.

He gave her a once-over as she slipped into the front seat. The alarm continued to ring, and now, Ella spotted a flashing light from one of the office buildings centering the junkyard.

As her breath fogged the window at her side, the locks clicking, Ella glanced at her partner. "Your doing?"

Brenner nodded, putting the car in gear and pulling from their temporary parking spot. "You were taking too long," he said. "Figured maybe you needed a hand."

She gave a quick nod of gratitude, gripping the phone tightly in one hand.

"What's that?"

"Phone."

"I see that, thanks. What's it for?"

"Calling."

"Ella, are you there? Earth to Ella."

She blinked, glancing at him. "Sorry, what?"

He rolled his eyes, picking up speed as the tires made a similar motion. "What's on your mind? Did you find anything?"

"Yeah... yeah, I think so. This is the boss's phone," she said, wiggling it. "Unlocked."

Brenner's eyebrow quirked. "Nice job. So?"

"So I think we can find anyone he sold to. If he keeps some sort of record, and these money guys always do, we might be able to find who bought the gold."

"So not him? One of his?"

"He runs a tight ship. Security cameras. Armed guards. Plus he has an alibi. Not him."

"One of his men?"

"Possibly. But they wouldn't have been able to steal the gold. So there'd be a record of the purchase. And if they know the gold is diluted, why would they pay for it?"

"Good point."

Ella was now scrolling through the phone, frowning as she did, clicking on the file folder and then going to recent history.

Brenner watched her with a thoughtful expression, glancing between the phone and the road ahead. "Anything interesting?" he asked.

Ella's frown deepened. "Just a lot of calls to and from a number that's not saved in the contacts. Probably a burner phone. But there's no indication of who it belongs to."

"We'll have to trace it," Brenner said, his voice firm. "But for now, let's get this phone back to the station and see if we can dig up anything more."

Ella nodded, her eyes still focused on the screen. "There's one more thing," she said, holding up the phone to show Brenner the screen. "There's a text message that just came in."

Brenner took a quick glance before directing his attention back to the road. "What does it say?"

"It's just a location and a time. A meetup," Ella said, biting her lip as she read the message again.

Brenner's grip on the steering wheel tightened. "From the unknown number?"

"Yeah."

"Might be nothing."

"Might be."

Brenner frowned. "Might be connected. Any reason to think that number is important?"

"Yeah," Ella said, frowning. She continued to scroll through the messages. "He keeps texting weights."

"How's that?"

"Ounces. It's like... orders."

"So this unknown number is placing gold orders from our mobsters?"

"Don't think they're mob. But..."

Ella suddenly trailed off, staring.

"What is it?"

"I know the number."

"What? How?"

"Because," she said quietly, her voice tremoring. "It belongs to my dad."

Brenner turned to stare at her, but Ella just focused on the phone, frowning.

"Your dad?" Brenner cursed. "He just keeps popping up, doesn't he? Cilla didn't mention any business deals with these guys."

"No... maybe she didn't know."

"Maybe she was covering for your old man."

Ella scowled now, gripping the phone tightly. "Two-hundred ounces," she said. "That's his order. Almost half a million dollars."

Brenner whistled softly under his breath. They continued to pick up speed.

Ella just shook her head. "He does keep coming up, doesn't he?"

"Any noise from Graves?"

"Not in a while," she said. "He's probably still kicking over stones. Seeing what crawls out."

"Pretty sure he's what crawls out," muttered Brenner. "Think any of this has something to do with the Collective?" He wrinkled his nose as he said it, as if the whole business gave him a sour taste in his mouth. But Ella wasn't as offended by the term. She knew what existed in the hearts of humankind. She'd seen it far too often in her old job.

She shivered, shaking her head briefly. "I don't know. But I think we should take the meeting."

"You'll piss him off."

"He might have something to do with this."

"That's a lot of gold. Maybe your dad is selling it."

"I can guarantee he is," she said. "Anything for a profit. Especially if he knows it's diluted."

Brenner shook his head, frowning, glancing at her. "What was that address again?"

Chapter 11

The ice cave loomed before them like a gaping maw, its frozen teeth glinting menacingly in the dim light. The sound of dripping water echoed through the vast cavern, a sinister melody that only served to heighten the oppressive atmosphere. The cold air hung heavily around them, biting at their exposed skin and stealing the warmth from their breath as it mingled with the darkness.

"Quite a sight, isn't it?" The taxidermist's voice sliced through the silence. His gleaming, silver pendant dangling on his chest glowed under the scarce rays of light that managed to penetrate the depths of the cave. His dark coat and gloves gave him an air of menace, as if he were some malevolent specter come to haunt the icy halls. "Indeed," he murmured, replying to himself, stepping forward and allowing his gloved fingers to trace the contours of a particularly jagged icicle. "Nature is truly a master sculptor."

His eyes roamed over the frozen landscape, taking in every detail as though committing it to memory. As he moved further into the cave, his footsteps barely made a sound on the slick ice floor, leaving one to wonder how such a man could move so stealthily.

"Have you been here many times?" he asked, his voice low and slightly monotone, as if the cold had seeped into his bones and stolen his ability to emote.

"Ah, yes, a few times," came the reply from his own lips. But he paid it no heed, instead focusing on the way the ice seemed to contort and twist around itself, forming endless intricate patterns that reflected the eerie beauty of the cave.

He couldn't help but marvel at the macabre allure of the place, feeling a strange kinship with the frozen sculptures that surrounded him. It was as if they, too, had been caught in a moment of time, their beauty preserved for eternity. And he wondered, not for the first time, what it would be like to capture such beauty and hold it forever in his hands.

"Ah, well," he said finally, tearing his gaze away from the ice and turning back towards the entrance, where the faintest hint of sunlight still lingered. "We should keep moving, I suppose."

And so they pressed on, deeper into the heart of the cave, the darkness swallowing them whole as the sound of dripping water continued its mournful serenade.

He found the rest of his group only a few paces into the first cave. His eyes scanned the figures, moving past most of them to land on his *true* target.

The tour guide, a woman in her late twenties with long, brown hair cascading down her back, adjusted the straps of her backpack and took a deep breath. The cold air stung her lungs as she surveyed the group of tourists she was leading through the ice cave. She wore a red jacket that stood out like a beacon against the dark, frozen world around them.

"Please be careful," she instructed, her voice firm yet polite. "The icy floor can be quite slippery."

As the tourists cautiously moved further into the cave, the taxidermist approached the tour guide, his frame making him immediately stand out among the others. He glanced at the stalactites hanging overhead, seemingly entranced by their menacing beauty.

"Quite an interesting place you have here," he said, trying to engage her in conversation as he sidled up next to her. A few of the other tourists had cameras out and were taking pictures of the gleaming structures.

"Thank you," she replied, her tone professional and unflustered. Years of dealing with tourists had likely left her unshakable. "This ice cave is truly one of nature's masterpieces."

"Indeed," the taxidermist agreed, watching her closely. "You must have seen some incredible sights during your time as a tour guide."

Her eyes briefly flickered over to him, acknowledging his comment before returning to survey the rest of the group. "Yes, I've had the privilege."

"Yet you remain as composed and poised as ever," he observed, unable to keep a hint of admiration from creeping into his voice.

"Er, alright. Umm... Thank you," she responded, hesitant.

"Of course," the taxidermist murmured, seemingly satisfied with her response. He fell back slightly, allowing her to continue guiding the group further into the depths of the ice cave.

The ice cave seemed to hold its breath as the group moved deeper, the only sound being the soft crunch of their footsteps. The tour guide paused, her breath misting in the frigid air as she gestured towards an intricate array of icicles overhead. Her red jacket stood out vividly against the icy blue hues surrounding them.

He noticed this. The taxidermist, and his friends, noticed most things that communicated motion and grace.

"Take a moment to appreciate the delicate beauty of these formations," she advised, her voice warm and steady despite the cold. The tourists murmured in awe, snapping photos and whispering among themselves. "These have existed for nearly fifty thousand years," she said. "The oldest glacier we know of is nearly eight million years old." She flashed a smile.

The taxidermist lingered by her side, his head glistening under the dim lighting. He spoke softly, his monotone voice barely audible above the hushed conversations. "You move with such grace through this treacherous terrain. It's almost like watching a dancer."

The other tourists were still oohing and aahing and didn't overhear his comment.

The guide, however, cast him a wary glance. She shifted her weight, subtly putting more distance between them.

"Ah, so you do enjoy dancing then?" he asked, his dark eyes never leaving her face.

"I... not particularly, no," she answered hesitantly, her attention straying to the rest of the group to ensure they weren't venturing too far. "But we really should focus on the tour."

"Of course," he agreed, though he showed no intention of dropping the subject. "Do you prefer classical or modern styles?"

"Really, I don't have much time for it," she responded, clearly growing increasingly uncomfortable with the personal nature of his questions. He knew he was unnerving her, but he didn't mind. In a way, it almost appealed to him.

"Such a shame," he mused, leaning in closer. "Someone with your poise and elegance should be able to fully express themselves in dance."

"Excuse me," she interjected, her voice polite but firm as she sidestepped away from him. "I should check on the rest of the group." She hurried towards the other tourists, her hand clenching and unclenching at her side.

GIRL WHO FREEZES SHADOWS

"Everyone," she called out, her voice wavering only slightly. "Let's continue to the next chamber and see the sculptures there!"

The tourists began to file past her, moving further on. The taxidermist lingered back. He watched, waiting. Like she had in the entrance, the tour guide waited, counting one by one as the tour moved past her. She would be the last to exit.

He shifted his weight, slipping behind a pillar of ice, waiting.

She was glancing in his direction now but hadn't spotted him yet.

Her expression curdled into a frown. Her hand hovered near her phone, and her fingers touched against the device, which he could see outlined against her jacket pocket.

She took a few steps towards the back of the cavern. The rest of the tourists were now out of sight. As she stepped past his hiding spot, he moved.

"Wait," the taxidermist said, his voice cold and flat. He moved in front of her, blocking her path to the group of tourists.

She turned sharply, emitting a small gasp, her breath blossoming in the chill from the ice cave walls. His dark eyes bored into hers, unblinking and unyielding.

"Please move," she whispered, trying to push past him. Her gloved hands met the rough fabric of his dark coat, but it was like pushing against a wall. He didn't budge an inch, his thin frame deceptively strong.

"Answer me one question first," he insisted, still staring directly into her eyes. "Do you fear death?"

"Wha–" she stammered, taken aback by the sudden change in topic.

"Indulge me," he murmured, leaning closer. He could see flecks of ice on her dark coat, smell the stale dampness of the cave on her breath.

"Interesting," he mused, not moving. She was trapped, like a small animal cornered by a predator. His heart pounded in his ears, each beat echoing through the icy chamber. A musical rhythm. The same rhythms from childhood, from deep memory.

"Move," she demanded, panic creeping into her voice as she pushed against him again with all her strength. It was no use; he stood as solid as the ice surrounding them.

He smiled at her, flashing his teeth. Then, he reached out to snare her arm.

She yelped, stumbling back, eyes wide.

All attempts at professionalism vanished now at his touch. Panic flared through her gaze, horror as she spotted the way his eyes widened.

She let out a little, desperate gasp, then turned on her heel and ran in the opposite direction.

The fear had won. It so often did.

He smiled, briefly watching her as she sprinted through the icy labyrinth, her footsteps echoing off the frozen walls.

"Careful," he whispered. "It's slippery."

The cold air would now sting her lungs with each desperate breath, but she kept pushing herself, driven by the primal urge to escape.

She screamed over her shoulder. But the taxidermist remained eerily silent, his footsteps so light that they seemed to blend into the cracking ice beneath them. His stealth unnerved her; it was as if he were a ghost, haunting her every step.

"Leave me alone!" she yelled, her voice bouncing off the cave walls, shattering the fragile silence. She stumbled around a bend, almost colliding with a towering ice sculpture. The taxidermist barely noticed its beauty, the intricate patterns carved into the ice by countless years of dripping water.

"Such grace," he murmured from behind her, the first words he'd spoken since the chase began. "You move like a dancer."

Panting heavily, she continued to flee. He ran in pursuit and studied her movements like a scientist observing an experiment. It sent chills down his spine, knowing that he was imagining her lifeless body, posed and preserved like one of his stuffed animals.

"Think of how lovely you'll look," he whispered, his voice low and hypnotic. "Frozen in time, your beauty immortalized."

She pushed herself harder, the cave's twisting passages becoming a blur as she sped past them.

"Please, let me go!" she cried out, tears streaming down her face and freezing on her cheeks.

"Death comes for us all," he replied quietly, his words dripping with finality. He was barely breathing heavily at all.

The crunching sound of the taxidermist's boots against the ice, like teeth grinding on glass, reverberated through the cave, sending tremors down the tour guide's spine. Her breaths were frantic, her chest heaving as she gasped for air in the biting cold. She dared not look back, knowing that the eyes of the taxidermist would be locked onto her, unblinking and full of dark intent.

"Please!" she stammered, her voice trembling with desperation. "Somebody help me!"

Silence was her only answer, a suffocating shroud of quiet that hung between the stalactites above her head. The darkness swallowed her cries. They were far afield from the tourist group.

"Useless," the taxidermist whispered, his words an icy breeze against her neck. "No one can save you now."

"Help me!" she pleaded one last time, her voice barely audible over her own heavy breathing and the relentless pursuit of the taxidermist. "Please, someone... anyone... help me!"

Chapter 12

Night came faster than Ella would've liked, and now she felt exposed as she walked along the wharf, listening to the thrashing sound of the Bering Sea.

She peered ahead across the moldered wooden jetty, towards the small bait shop perched precariously on one side of the dock, tilting as if at any moment it might slip off into the freezing water.

She shivered again, involuntarily, rubbing her arms as she moved hastily forward.

The moon cast a silvery glow on the dark fisherman's wharf, muted by the heavy clouds above. The frigid Alaskan wind whipped around Ella as she made her way carefully over the half-frozen water that surrounded the dock. Nome was fast approaching winter, and the air held the scent of salt and fish, mingled with the faintest hint of decay. In the distance, the wind seemed to whisper, reminding her that she wasn't on her own.

She paused, glancing over her shoulder, surveying the elevated ridge where a slew of shops were set up, but closed for the night.

She couldn't see him, but Brenner was on one of those roofs. Overwatch.

Her father had never approved much of Brenner Gunn, and so Ella had insisted he stay behind.

In response, the ex-SEAL sniper had insisted they stop by his apartment to snatch a rifle so he could keep an eye on things.

She couldn't see him, but it felt nice to know she had her own guardian angel somewhere behind her.

She returned her attention to the bait shop where her father had set the meeting with the drug-dealing gold-runner. He wasn't expecting her.

Which meant things could go one of two ways.

Ella's heart pounded in her chest, her breath visible in the icy air. She glanced back again, and this time she spotted a whisper of movement. She wouldn't have, she knew, if he hadn't wanted her too. Brenner's position was strategic, nestled between stacks of fishing crates and an abandoned trawler, offering an unobstructed view of the entire wharf while remaining virtually undetectable.

As Ella approached the designated meeting spot, she couldn't shake the feeling that she was being watched by more than one set of eyes. The darkness seemed to close in around her, filled with the whispers of the past. This place had once been bustling with life and commerce, but now it stood as a monument to a bygone era, swallowed by the inexorable tide of time.

Her father, Jameson, was a gold tycoon in Nome—a man who built his fortune on the backs of others. A tall, handsome man with the deceptive charm of a politician. He was also danger-ous, and Ella knew that any encounter with him could very well be her last. But she had questions that needed answers, and there was only one person who could provide them.

"Stay sharp," she whispered into her radio receiver tucked inside her lapel, knowing Brenner was ready to spring into action at a moment's notice. "Keep an eye out for anything unusual."

"Copy that," came the terse reply, Brenner's voice barely au-dible over the wind.

As she neared the edge of the dock, Ella's senses were on high alert. The darkness was oppressive, but her eyes had adjust-ed enough to make out the shapes of fishing boats moored nearby, gently rocking with the movement of the water. She focused on each sound and shadow, desperate for some sign of her father's presence. But all she found was silence—a suffocating, unnerving silence that weighed heavily on her shoulders.

"Where are you?" she murmured, anxiety gnawing at the edges of her resolve. She knew that her father was a man who thrived in the shadows, and this meeting was simply another game of cat and mouse. But she couldn't afford to lose, not when so much was at stake.

And as she took another step into the darkness, it felt as though the entire world was holding its breath.

Ella's own breaths came in shallow and quick, her boots crunching on the frosty dock as she moved forward. Her hands were cold despite the gloves, clutching her weapon tightly. She scanned the area, eyes darting from one shadowy corner to another. Nothing seemed out of place—a few boats bobbed up and down in the murky water while ropes creaked and groaned against the wooden poles.

"Still no sign of him," she muttered under her breath, her voice barely audible over the sound of the wind. It whipped around her, carrying with it the stench of salt and decaying fish. She shivered involuntarily, pressing onward.

"Stay focused, Ella," Brenner's voice whispered in her ear. "You spot any danger, and I'll come."

"No... no, that's fine."

"Be patient," he said. "No sense rushing anything. He doesn't know who's coming, remember?"

But her patience was wearing thin, and all she had were the thoughts running through her head, filling her with doubt and uncertainty. The silence was stifling, interrupted only by her own heartbeat pounding in her ears.

Suddenly, three figures emerged from the darkness, cutting through the fog like specters, having waited until she nearly came in line with the door of the bait shop. Their movements were swift and coordinated as they surrounded her, guns aimed at her chest. Ella's heart skipped a beat, instincts taking over as she raised her weapon.

"Easy now," one of the gunmen said, his voice deep and gravelly. He stepped closer, face partially obscured by a black ski mask. "Viktor send you?"

Instead of answering his question, she offered one of her own. "Who are you?" Ella demanded, her voice steady despite the fear threatening to choke her. She tried her best to keep her gaze fixed on all three men, but her focus kept drifting back to the two men still standing in the doorway. Their forms were unmistakable. Thickset, no necks, dull eyes. She recognized them as her father's bodyguards, their expressions cold and unreadable.

"Take it easy, Ms. Porter." The second bodyguard spoke up, his words clipped and business-like. "You ain't supposed to be here."

He recognized her.

This gave her a unique opportunity. Ella paused, cleared her throat, then said, imitating her sister's no-nonsense ways as much as possible, "Take me to him. Now! It's about the business."

The two men shared a look. One of them hesitated, glancing at her again.

"Your dad ain't expecting you," said the first one, slowly.

"Is that what this is?" Ella asked, her voice laced with sarcasm. "A family reunion?"

"Nah..." the man trailed off after this bit of witty repartee.

"Fine," Ella said, lowering her weapon slowly. "Just remember, I'm not here to cause trouble."

The third gunman was talking into a radio receiver. "Yeah, your daughter, sir. Which one?" He glanced at Ella. "Does she have pierced ears?" He leaned in, studying her ears, his breath hot on her face, smelling of cigarettes.

Then he withdrew. "Nah. No earrings."

Ella winced, absentmindedly touching her ear.

Before she could say anything, though, two thugs flanked her and began pushing and prodding at her.

As they led her away from the dock, each step taking her deeper into uncertainty, Ella couldn't help but wonder if maybe this time she'd bitten off more than she could chew.

"You good?" came Brenner's voice in her ear.

She coughed, covering a quick reply, "Fine."

When one of the guards glanced at her, she shrugged. "Fine. Take me to him. Let's go."

The gunmen led Ella down a narrow alley created by the bait shop and a walkway leading under the dock. The smell of damp and rusted metal lingered in the air. As they approached a black-tinted SUV parked at a boat launching area, her heart pounded in her chest like a caged animal. The vehicle was large and imposing, with thick tires that gripped the frost-covered ground beneath it, tilted vaguely on the incline leading to the frosted coast. The SUV seemed to consume the faint moonlight that struggled to illuminate the scene.

"Get in," one of the gunmen said, opening the rear door for her. Ella hesitated for only a moment before stepping inside, knowing that to resist would be futile—and possibly fatal.

As she slid into the cold leather seat, she found herself face-to-face with Jameson Porter, her father.

And for a moment, it was as if time stopped.

He was tall and broad-shouldered, his salt-and-pepper hair immaculately styled as always. His eyes, a piercing blue that mirrored her own, bore into her with an intensity that made her shiver. Even seated, he exuded an aura of power and control that was impossible to deny.

"Ah, Ella," he said, his voice smooth and confident, like a seasoned politician. "I must say, I didn't expect to see you here tonight."

"Neither did I," Ella replied, struggling to keep her voice steady. She tore her gaze from his, focusing on the dimly lit streets outside the window instead. "But here I am."

"Indeed." Jameson leaned back against the plush upholstery, studying her carefully. "I was... expecting someone else. I assume my business partner won't be showing up tonight?"

"It's unlikely," she replied.

Her father sighed and shook his head, folding his hands on his lap. She knew better than to take in his relaxed posture as anything but camouflage. She'd seen her father switch from calm and reserved to downright rageful in a matter of nanoseconds.

Ella couldn't help but feel a chill crawl up her spine as she realized how precarious her position had become. If she played her cards wrong, she might not make it out of the SUV alive.

"Speaking of business," she said finally, forcing herself to meet his gaze. "I'm investigating some... issues."

"Interesting." Jameson's eyes narrowed slightly, and Ella could see the gears turning in his mind. "And what kind of issues would those be?"

"Gold," she replied, trying not to let her fear show in her voice. "Specifically, diluted gold."

"Ah, I see." Jameson leaned forward, his expression unreadable. "And how, pray tell, does that concern me?"

Ella swallowed hard, her pulse racing as she realized that this was the moment of truth—the point of no return.

"Because," she said softly, her heart pounding against her ribcage, "I believe you might know something about it."

For a moment, the only sound in the SUV was their ragged breathing, their breaths mingling in the cold night air.

"Is that so?" Jameson asked, his tone deceptively mild. "Well, then, we'd better talk."

Ella braced herself, her fingers curling into fists. She chose her words carefully, her tone steady and measured. "I have reason to believe that your company has been purchasing diluted gold. I need to know who you're buying it from, and where these transactions are taking place."

Jameson raised an eyebrow, his features a mask of impassiveness. He regarded her for a moment as if weighing her worth and the potential risks she posed. Finally, he leaned back in his seat, steepling his fingers.

"Very well," he said, his voice barely above a whisper. "I'll admit that I have many business ventures. And if I buy crude gold, it's only a small portion of our overall operations but profitable nonetheless."

Ella could feel a mixture of relief and dread wash over her. Relief that her father was willing to share information and dread at the thought of what this revelation might mean for her investigation.

"Who do you deal with?" she asked, trying to keep her voice level.

"His name is Viktor," Jameson replied. "Sometimes. Other times he goes by other names. A businessman with ties to several... organizations. He operates out of a junkyard on the outskirts of Nome. Only a select few have access to that location—Viktor himself, his trusted associates, and a handful of representatives from the companies he deals with." Her father leaned forward now. "But you undoubtedly knew all of this before coming here. So why don't you cut to the chase. What are you really after?"

"I want to know who you sell the diluted gold to."

"I see." Jameson acknowledged her comment with a nod. "Let me make one thing clear, Ella. My involvement with Viktor and his operation is purely business. The diluted gold isn't directly connected to anything untoward. I like to keep things legal." He flashed a crocodile smile that looked like it belonged in a political ad.

She hesitated only briefly. With a man like her father, bluff would be met with bluff. Sometimes, the best approach was a direct one. Besides, her ear was itching from how much Brenner was whispering, making sure she was still alright.

So Ella said, her voice barely audible, "The gold you purchased was found in the eye sockets of a corpse."

"The ice caves?" her father asked.

She blinked. "You know about that murder?"

"This is Nome, my dear. I know a lot."

"Do you know who would've purchased that gold? Someone with experience in taxidermy."

"Taxidermy?" Her father's eyebrows inched up. "How utterly morbid and fascinating." He steepled his fingers, studying her for a long moment. He pressed his lips tightly together. Then, at last, he said, "You know what... perhaps you and I can help each other."

She blinked. "Oh?"

"Yes. Maybe... just maybe, we are at cross-purposes." He flashed another smile. His eyes were still cold. "But I am a businessman, dear. You know this. Information isn't cheap. I'm only willing to share it with you if you do something for me first. As far as I can tell, you owe me a favor or two after the meddling you've been involved with."

Ella hesitated. The way her father's eyes bore into hers made her uneasy, but she knew she couldn't pass up any information that could help her investigation. "What do you want?" She decided not to comment on the accusation of *meddling*.

"Find someone for me," Jameson replied, his voice as smooth and dangerous as ever. "A man who goes by the name of the Architect."

Ella went still.

He nodded suddenly. "Ah, I see. So you *do* know the name."

She kept her expression a mask. "Who is it?"

He just watched her.

"I can't find someone if you don't tell me who they are."

"Hmm... Do we have to play this game, daughter? There was a time we could cooperate."

Ella didn't remember such a time, but decided now wasn't the moment to point it out. She was too worried about ending up under the ice, a bullet lodged in her skull.

"So who is the Architect?" she said, trying not to think too much about what Mortimer Graves had told her about the eccentric and enigmatic billionaire who ran the Collective.

Her father crossed his legs slowly, his hands resting on each other.

"An enigmatic figure who specializes in designing intricate criminal networks," Jameson explained. "A truly depraved individual. The sort that the FBI *should* be spending their resources on." His eyebrows inched up.

"And what do you want with him?" she said.

"I'm a concerned citizen," he replied, flashing a quick smile.

Ella paused, glancing out the window. The three guards were still walking along the jetty. Another guard was sitting in the driver's seat.

She paused, hesitant. Then her eyes widened. "Are you scared?" she blurted out.

Her father's eyes narrowed.

"You've made enemies," she said, nodding quickly. "With this Architect?"

He just watched her. "I'm not asking you to arrest him. Just to find him," her father said.

"Oh? And then what do you plan on doing?"

"A little chat," her father said.

"I saw your journal," she replied. "The blackmail you keep. You have a way of finding things. Why not find him?"

Her father frowned at the mention of the journal, but he didn't comment on it. Perhaps because he'd already known of her involvement, or because he didn't want her to know he hadn't.

Instead, he retorted, "Because he's elusive. Like a ghost," Jameson replied, frustration evident in his expression. "I've tried. Believe me. But my resources have come up empty-handed. You, on the other hand, have a certain... talent for finding people who don't want to be found. And connections." He shrugged. "Besides, I'm busy here... You're uniquely situated."

Ella swallowed hard, weighing her options. Her mind raced with thoughts of what this favor might cost her. She needed to know who'd purchased the gold. Who'd killed that woman.

Besides, she *wanted* to find the Architect herself, didn't she?

"Fine," she agreed, trying to steady her breathing. "I'll find the Architect for you. But you better hold up your end of the bargain."

"Of course, dear," Jameson said with a cold smile. "I always keep my promises."

"Then tell me where to find the gold purchaser," Ella demanded, her voice firm despite the fear that clawed at her insides.

"Patience," Jameson admonished. "First things first. The Architect is a master at hiding in plain sight. He's rumored to have eyes and ears everywhere. You'll need to be cautious and discreet. He works for... an organization that takes it personal when people meddle."

There was that word again... *meddling.* She wondered how close her father was to simply ending it there. She knew he was the type to hold a grudge, but he was a businessman. He wouldn't waste an asset, no matter how distasteful.

Things really had changed between them.

She wondered what a normal Christmas or Thanksgiving would have been like.

"I'll look into it," she said simply. "You have my word."

Her father studied her then nodded. "Your word. I'll accept that. Hopefully, the check doesn't bounce."

"So?" she said. "The gold resale?"

"Ah, yes... Now that's simple enough, dear. I only have one purchaser."

She stared at him.

"Only the one. Most people won't purchase diluted gold. And I'm certainly not going to tarnish my reputation by selling it undeclared."

"So... so the buyer *knows* it's not pure?"

"They requested as much. Said it was needed for a special project."

"And who is he?"

"She," her father said, flashing a wolfish smile. "Dr. Tulip Messer," he said simply.

Ella stared. Dr. Messer was the coroner in Nome. She was a grandmotherly sort but with connections to Ella's father. Also, Dr. Messer was a big game hunter who liked to stuff her own animals and display them in the cabins she kept in the mountains.

Ella frowned, her brow low.

"Dr. Messer buys the gold?"

"Quite," her father said. "Now... remember your side of the deal."

"I remember. You're sure? Only Dr. Messer?"

Her father waved a finger over his heart. "Cross my heart... and hope to..."

He smirked.

Die, she thought, finishing the expression.

Ella shivered as she pushed out of the car, expecting a bullet in the spine at any moment. But it never came.

She didn't stop moving until she reached the end of the wharf. She could feel eyes watching her.

Eyes from every direction.

Then, breathing in shallow puffs, Ella broke into a jog, racing back towards where she'd left Brenner.

It was getting late.

But Dr. Messer often kept odd hours due to her morning hunting schedule.

Ella felt a shiver. She didn't like the idea of visiting a coroner at night.

But sometimes, her personal preferences only got in the way.

Chapter 13

The moon hung heavy in the sky, casting a silver sheen over the world. Ella stood beneath its glow, her heart hammering in her chest as she glanced at Brenner Gunn. His eyes locked onto hers—a silent signal that it was now or never.

"Ready?" he whispered, his voice barely audible. Ella nodded, her determination steeling her nerves. She had always been one to follow her instincts, and they had never failed her before. But Dr. Tulip Messer? The grandmotherly coroner was an odd duck for sure, but hardly a killer... Well, this wasn't strictly true. Ella had seen evidence of the kills Messer had bagged while on hunting trips in the mountains.

But as far as law-breaking?

The only things that came close to criminal were the rock-hard cookies that Messer sometimes offered.

Now, though, she didn't know what to think.

Together, Ella and Brenner cautiously approached the coroner's office, their shadows stretching out behind them like dark extensions of their bodies. The door loomed before them, a barrier separating secrets from those seeking answers. With a swift, deft motion, Brenner produced a lockpick from his pocket, tension wrench already in place. Within seconds, the door clicked open, allowing them passage into the realm of the dead.

Silence enveloped them as they stepped inside, the air thick with the scent of formaldehyde and stale coffee. Ella felt the goosebumps rise on her arms, an involuntary shiver making its way down her spine. The darkness seemed to press in on them from all sides, but they remained undeterred, moving forward with purpose.

"Watch where you step," Ella murmured, her voice hushed to match the quietude of their surroundings. "We don't want to wake the dead."

"Or alert the living," Brenner added, his words underscored by the faintest hint of humor. He pulled a small flashlight from his pocket, clicking it on and directing its beam towards the floor. They navigated the maze of examination tables and equipment with practiced ease, each step calculated and precise.

As Ella moved through the dimly lit space, her mind raced with the possibilities of what they might uncover. What secrets did Dr. Messer keep hidden within these walls? It was a question that had plagued her ever since her father's information had fallen into her lap, and she was determined to find the answer.

"Over there," Brenner whispered, pointing towards a door at the far end of the room. "That's her office."

"Don't think she's here," Ella replied, her voice carrying the weight of their shared mission. She held her breath as they crossed the remaining distance, anticipation coiling in her gut like a snake poised to strike.

As they reached the door, Ella felt her heartbeat quicken, the thrill of breaking new ground electrifying her senses. They were closer than ever to uncovering the truth, and with each step, the pieces of the puzzle began to fall into place.

"Ready?" Brenner asked once more, his eyes searching hers for any sign of hesitation.

"Absolutely," Ella said, her voice steady and unwavering. Maybe her father had been lying? Then again, she'd always known he'd been friendly with the coroner. But as his sole purchaser of diluted gold?

She had to find *something*.

With one last look at each other, they pushed open the door and stepped inside, ready to confront whatever lay hidden in the depths of the coroner's office.

Inside, Ella's gaze immediately fell upon an unsettling sight: past the desk, and the sparsely furnished, bare floor, she spotted a mantlepiece above an empty slot in the wall. And on the mantlepiece...

She stifled a small breath, staring, her eyes narrowing.

A collection of taxidermy animals perched on shelves and lining the walls. Each specimen appeared meticulously preserved, their polished claws and teeth reflecting the faint light that seeped into the room. Except something was off. As she looked closer, Ella realized that all of the eyes were missing, leaving empty sockets where they should have been.

"Look at this," Ella whispered to Brenner, her voice betraying a hint of unease. "All the eyes are gone."

"Creepy," Brenner agreed, casting his own wary glance over the macabre menagerie. "What do you think it means?

"Could be a clue," Ella mused, her instincts taking over despite the disturbing nature of the discovery. She thought of the golden eyes in their victim... it couldn't be a coincidence, could it? "Let's search the room. Maybe there's something here..."

Brenner hesitated, glancing at her.

The two of them both shared an uncomfortable look, likely thinking along the same lines.

"You don't... don't think she actually had something to do with this, do you?" he muttered.

She couldn't quite meet Brenner's gaze. Instead, she sighed and shook her head. "I don't know what to think," she murmured. And she moved towards the desk.

They split up, scouring the office with practiced efficiency. Ella rifled through drawers and cabinets, her nimble fingers sifting through files and documents, searching for any scrap of evidence that might point them in the right direction. Meanwhile, Brenner inspected the taxidermy animals more closely, hoping to find some trace of something... *anything* hidden among the lifeless creatures.

As Ella worked, her mind raced with possibilities. Perhaps Dr. Messer had a morbid fascination with eyes, or maybe the gaps in the taxidermy display held some deeper significance. She knew the truth could be lurking anywhere.

"Find anything?" Ella asked Brenner, breaking the silence that had settled over the room like a heavy fog.

"Nothing yet," he replied, frustration evident in his voice. "It's like looking for a needle in a haystack. What exactly are we looking for? Creepy? Check. Weird taxidermy? Also check? An 'I did it' note from a killer? Not so much."

"Keep searching," Ella urged him, unwilling to give up so easily. "There has to be *something.*"

"Right," Brenner muttered, returning to his search, this time analyzing the teeth of the animals as if checking for food residue.

As the minutes ticked by, Ella's focus sharpened, her eyes darting from one coroner file to another. The weight of what they were doing settled on her shoulders like an invisible cloak, but she refused to let it slow her down.

It was as she rummaged through the last drawer that her attention was caught by a sudden sound.

A creaking noise.

Ella's breath caught in her throat at the sound of a groaning floorboard outside the office door. Her heart pounded as if it were trying to escape her chest, and she instinctively reached for the gun holstered at her waist.

"Stay back," she whispered to Brenner.

The office door swung open, revealing Dr. Messer standing in the doorway, a shotgun pointed directly at them. The dim light from the hallway cast eerie shadows on her face, making her expression unreadable. She had weathered, wrinkled features in an otherwise pleasant face. White curls framed her aged features. She was wearing camo pants and a white lab coat.

"Hands where I can see them!" Dr. Messer barked, her voice cold and commanding, leaving no room for argument.

Ella thought for a split second but then complied, and Brenner followed suit, both raising their hands slowly into the air. Ella's mind raced as she tried to come up with something to say.

"Dr. Messer, we—" Ella began, only to be cut off by the doctor's sharp tone.

"Quiet! Wait... Hang on..." The coroner wrinkled her nose suddenly, leaning in and blinking a few times as her eyes adjusted from the dark hall to the suddenly illuminated room. Then, her painted-on eyebrows inched towards her white fringe.

As Dr. Messer studied their faces, the hostile look in her eyes softened, and she lowered her weapon with a sudden sigh. "Ella Porter and Brenner Gunn? What are you two doing here?"

"Umm... looking around," Ella said cautiously, her mind whirring as she attempted to make sense of the situation.

"For what?" Messer said, sounding genuinely bemused.

Ella could feel her stomach twisting into odd shapes. Now that she was face to face with the familiar coroner, she simply couldn't *see* it. This woman wasn't a killer, was she?

Ella studied Dr. Messer's face, searching for any signs of deception. But then, she blurted out, "You bought gold from my father. The same type of gold was discovered in a taxidermy victim in the ice caves." She didn't continue, preferring to let the words imply everything she was thinking.

Messer blinked a couple of times, but then her eyes widened.

"Oh," she said. She glanced at her own animals on the mantlepiece. "Oh..." she said, her voice tightening. Her lips pressed into a small circle, forming thin lines. "I see..."

Ella remained quiet.

Dr. Messer let out a long sigh. "Hmm... Gold, you say? In the eyes?"

"Yes."

"Crude gold? Impure stuff?"

"That's right."

Messer sighed now, leaning here shotgun against the door and stepping into her office. She patted Ella's shoulder in a sort of comforting way as she scooted past and approached the mantlepiece.

She moved towards the very edge of the mantlepiece and turned a small squirrel towards them.

This one, unlike the others, still had its eyes, though its tail was missing.

"Fine," Dr. Messer said with a resigned sigh, stroking the squirrel behind the ears. "I suppose I owe you an explanation. You see, my taxidermy work isn't exactly... traditional." Her fingers brushed over the surface of a nearby specimen, the golden sheen catching Ella's attention.

"Is that... gold?" Brenner questioned, stepping closer to examine the intricate details of the squirrel's eyes.

"Yes," Dr. Messer admitted, a hint of pride seeping into her voice. "I've developed a unique technique using crude gold to create lifelike eyes for my creations. It's become quite popular at hunter conventions."

Ella raised an eyebrow. "And these conventions... are they exclusive to professionals like yourself?"

"Indeed," Dr. Messer replied. "It's a gathering of the best in the field, where we exchange ideas and techniques, as well as showcase our latest works."

Brenner nodded thoughtfully, his gaze still fixed on the gilded creature. "If your work is so highly regarded, why keep it hidden away here?"

"Because," Dr. Messer hesitated, her expression darkening, "someone stole the golden eyes from my newest collection. I have no idea who could have done it or why, but I can't risk exposing the rest of my work until I find out. It's why I'm here with that," she added, nodding at the shotgun by the door. "I had a motion detector installed on my office door. I thought the thief had returned." Suddenly, her eyes narrowed, and she glance between them. "You two didn't take my gold, did you?"

"No," Brenner said simply.

"Absolutely not," Ella replied. Ella's mind had begun to race with the new information, trying to piece together the puzzle. If someone had stolen the golden eyes, it was possible they were connected to the murders. But if Dr. Messer was telling the truth, then she herself wasn't involved.

"Dr. Messer," Ella began, her voice low and serious, "we need your help. If there's a connection between the stolen eyes and these crimes, we have to find it before more lives are lost. And the only way to move on... And I hate to ask you... but we need an alibi for the last couple of nights."

Dr. Messer looked at Ella for a moment, weighing her options. Finally, she nodded in agreement. "Alright. I was at home with my grand-daughters making sugar cookies. I have pictures." She smiled. "And videos. And witnesses. Is that enough? I'm just a coroner but... feels like that should work, hmm?"

At the twinkle in Dr. Messer's eyes, Ella felt a flicker of relief.

"I can show you if you let me grab my phone from my purse."

"Deal," Ella said firmly, gesturing her hand towards the door.

Dr. Messer retreated and then returned a second later, carrying her phone. It took the older woman a few minutes to boot up the device, but once she did, she turned it so they could see.

Ella checked the dates on the cute images of Messer and her grandkids making sugar cookies, and she found herself inhaling in slow relief.

"We good?" Brenner said, addressing the question to Ella.

She double checked the video. "Yeah. We're good."

Brenner seemed to relax, and Messer smiled, stowing her phone slowly, while still wearing a quizzical expression.

Ella, on the other hand, was frowning again.

"Dr. Messer," Ella said, her eyes scanning the room, "you mentioned your success at hunter conventions. When and where was the most recent one?"

Dr. Messer leaned against the doorframe, folding her arms across her chest. She seemed to relax a bit, her shoulders dropping, as she realized that Ella was genuinely seeking her help.

"Three weeks ago, in Anchorage," Dr. Messer replied, her voice still a touch defensive. "I even won first place with my latest creation."

Ella breathed a small sigh of relief, her muscles relaxing just a hair. At least they could rule out Dr. Messer as a suspect. But there was still so much to uncover. Her mind raced, thoughts shifting like quicksilver as she contemplated their next move.

"Did you notice anything unusual at the convention?" Ella asked, her gaze locked on Dr. Messer's face, searching for any hint of falsehood or deception. "Anyone who seemed particularly interested in your work, or perhaps someone new?"

"Nothing out of the ordinary," Dr. Messer answered, narrowing her eyes as she thought back. "Just the usual crowd of collectors and enthusiasts. Though, now that you mention it..."

She trailed off, her brow furrowing as she dug into her memory. Ella leaned in, eager to catch any scrap of information that might help them piece together the puzzle.

"There was a man," Dr. Messer continued slowly, "a stranger. I didn't recognize him from previous conventions. He spent quite a bit of time at my booth, asking questions about my process, my materials. At the time, I didn't think much of it—people are always curious about the craftsmanship behind taxidermy art."

"What did he look like?" Ella pressed, her heart pounding with a mix of excitement and trepidation.

"Middle-aged, tall, balding," Dr. Messer recalled, her eyes distant as she painted the picture in her mind. "He wore thick glasses and had a bit of a stoop to his shoulders."

"Did he give you a name?" Ella asked, her fingers itching for a pen and paper to jot down the details.

"A... something," Dr. Messer said, shaking her head as if to dislodge the elusive memory. "I'm sorry, I can't remember."

"Every detail helps," Ella reassured her, determination stoking the fire in her chest. The connection between the stolen eyes and the murders was still foggy, but she could feel the pieces starting to come together.

"If it helps, the next convention is tomorrow," said Messer with a shrug. "This one in Juneau."

Ella looked up, alert. "That's where you were planning on showcasing these creations?" she asked, waving a hand towards the animals on the mantlepiece.

"Exactly. But I can't until I get more gold." Messer sighed.

"Thank you, Dr. Messer," Ella said, her gaze unwavering as she processed the information. "I suppose we only have one recourse."

"Oh? And what is that, dearie?"

"We'll be attending the convention tomorrow to investigate further."

"Take care, Detective Porter," Dr. Messer replied, a shadow of concern crossing her face. "Some of the types won't like it if they know you're federal."

"Will do."

Brenner glanced around the room once more, adjusted some papers on the desk, then nodded to Messer and moved out of the door.

Ella gave the coroner a sheepish look, wincing apologetically.

Dr. Messer sighed, gathered herself, but then flashed a quick smile and a wink.

Ella returned the smile, feeling a bit lighter.

"Better get going," said Messer. "I came running with cookies still in the oven when the motion sensor was triggered. I need to go."

With a nod, Ella bid farewell, feeling much lighter in spirit than when she'd first entered the office, and she turned on her heel and left the coroner's office, Brenner following close behind.

The night air was cold against Ella's cheeks as they made their way back to their car. She couldn't shake the nagging feeling that they were onto something significant, the thread of a tangled web finally beginning to unravel.

"Are you sure about going to the convention?" Brenner asked, his brow furrowed with concern.

"I have to," Ella replied, her voice firm. "Someone saw those golden eyes. Stole them from Messer."

"You believe that story?"

Ella paused, nodded. "Yes. I do. She had an alibi." Ella was going to add more when her phone beeped.

She frowned, glanced down, and then froze.

"What is it?" Brenner said. "Ella?"

She stared at the message, feeling a cold chill along her spine. It was night, now. Nearly eight PM. Not even a full day had passed since they'd taken the case.

And now this.

She read the text message aloud this time. *They found another body."*

Chapter 14

The taxidermist stood at a distance from the ice caves, his feet planted firmly in the snow-covered ground as his breath fogged up the binoculars. He adjusted the focus, tracking the movement of the cars and the flashing of the lights with a predatory gleam in his eyes. The chaos unfolding before him was like a well-choreographed dance; each car swerving and skidding, headlights illuminating the darkness, all contributing to the symphony of violence that thrilled him.

"Ah, music to my ears," he whispered, grinning wickedly. As the sound of screeching tires and shattering glass filled the air, he became lost in the music of his own mind. His finger began to wave around like a conductor's wand, orchestrating the destruction below. He moved it slowly at first, tracing the trajectory of a car as it pulled over to the side of the road leading to the ice caves.

"More!" he demanded, his voice barely audible against the cacophony of chaos. He swept his hand to the side, envisioning an explosion of glass and metal as two cars collided, slipping on the ice, an ambulance ramming into the rear of a police cruiser. The taxidermist's movements grew more frantic, his entire body caught up in the physicality of his imaginary symphony. With every crash and scream, his excitement mounted, driving him further into his obsession with violence.

"Bravo! Bravo!" he shouted into the night, his finger slashing through the air to punctuate each imagined crescendo. There was power here, he thought, in being the master of this mayhem. For a moment, he felt untouchable, invincible, as though the world was his to control.

And yet, as the last echoes of destruction faded away, he realized it wasn't enough. He needed more – another to satisfy the hunger gnawing at his insides. The taxidermist's finger stilled, the music in his mind silenced by the urgency of his twisted desires. Slowly, deliberately, he lowered the binoculars.

As beads of sweat formed on his forehead, the taxidermist felt himself consumed by the crescendo in his mind. His breathing grew heavy and labored, each exhale a guttural accompaniment to the symphony playing out before him. He wiped away the perspiration with the back of his hand, feeling the cold air sting his damp skin.

"Ah, yes," he murmured, his eyes widening at the sight of the chaos below. "Perfect."

His finger continued to wave through the air, directing the mayhem as if it were an orchestra of sirens, flashing lights, and law enforcement officers. The corners of his mouth twitched into the ghost of a smile, betraying his delight. A low chuckle rumbled in his chest, swelling with each new act of frantic desperation.

"Look," he said softly, addressing the audience only he could see. "Look at what we have created together. Mother, do you see now? I told you I'd do it! I told you! More!" he whispered, his voice hoarse with anticipation. "Give me more!"

As the final chords of his imaginary symphony began to fade, the taxidermist's fervor subsided, leaving him breathless and wanting. He knew that this was just the beginning—that his insatiable appetite for chaos would lead him down a path lined with frigid bodies and dancer delights.

A smile began to stretch across the taxidermist's face, slow and deliberate, like ink seeping through a porous surface. The corners of his mouth curled upwards, exposing teeth that glinted in the dim light. His eyes, wide and unblinking, were filled with a predatory gleam as they continued to follow the pandemonium below.

His fingers twitched involuntarily, itching to join the fray, to grasp and mold the mayhem into a twisted work of art.

"Perhaps it's time for another masterpiece," he mused, his voice low and hungry. "But who will be my muse this time, Mother? Who?"

He knew he needed to choose carefully, to find the perfect specimen for his dark desires. Or mother would *not* be happy. It had to be someone who would appreciate the beauty in the chaos, who would embrace the pain and suffering with open arms.

"Ah, there you are," he breathed, his eyes locking onto a figure struggling to emerge from the car wedged against a snowbank.

A pretty blonde woman who moved with a confidence that belied her petite size.

His heart raced with excitement as he envisioned the process of immortalizing his new muse. The careful preservation of their final moments, the delicate manipulation of their limbs to create the perfect tableau of agony and despair—it was an art form that he had perfected over the years, one that brought him a twisted sense of satisfaction and pride.

"Patience," he reminded himself, taking a step back from the edge of his vantage point. "All good things come to those who wait."

The icy wind whipped through the taxidermist's hair, its cold fingers caressing his skin as he stood hidden in the shadows. The howling gusts were like a chorus of voices in his ears, each one crying out for mercy or salvation. He reveled in the sensation.

With every beat of the imaginary orchestra, the taxidermist felt his anticipation grow stronger. His fingers twitched with the desire to wield his tools, to carve and shape the flesh of his chosen victim into a frozen tableau of suffering. He envisioned the haunting expressions he would craft, the twisted limbs arranged in the most exquisite display of agony. It was all so clear in his mind, synchronized with the macabre music that filled his soul.

"Soon, very soon," he whispered, his voice barely audible above the howling wind. "We shall create our magnum opus, you and I." He stared at the pretty blonde woman, his binoculars fixated on her. He found himself breathing heavily as he watched her.

He could almost see the ghostly figures of the dancers who populated his inner world, their skeletal hands moving gracefully over their instruments. They were the unsung heroes of his grisly art, providing the soundtrack that fueled his obsession with violence and chaos.

"Patience, my friends," he told them, his eyes never leaving the scene of destruction below. "Our time will come. And it will be glorious."

The taxidermist's finger, now a violent baton, slashed through the air in frenetic harmony with his mind's music. The crescendo was building, and he could feel the sweat beading on his brow as he guided the phantom orchestra through its morbid symphony.

His heart pounded in time to the heavy percussion as he furiously waved his hand, orchestrating every note of chaos that unfolded before him. In the midst of his fevered conducting, his eyes never strayed from the scene below.

The sirens in the distance grew louder, their discordant wail mingling with the somber tones of his private concert. But the taxidermist remained unfazed, hypnotized by the music in his head and his imperviousness to the suffering around him.

"Can't you hear it?" he asked the wind, his voice tinged with a hint of madness. "The most beautiful melody of all, woven from pain and chaos. Bravo!" he cried, his voice carried away by the gusts of wind, as he allowed the final notes of his imaginary symphony to fade away into the night.

His eyes were drawn back to the pretty blonde lady once more.

Then, he turned the binoculars to the car, taking in the license plate.

He'd follow her home. Yes... yes, that would be the best decision.

To wait.

To follow.

And then to strike.

Chapter 15

The frosty air stung Ella's cheeks as she stepped into the dimly lit cavern, her breath visible in the icy atmosphere.

Ella's fingers hesitated above her phone screen as she composed a quick text message, the glare from her device casting an eerie glow on her face amidst the ice cave's dim lighting. "Maddie, sorry but I might have to postpone dinner tonight. Investigating a crime scene in the caves. Will let you know ASAP. -E" She hit send and slipped the phone back into her pocket, feeling a pang of guilt for yet another likely cancellation. But it couldn't be helped; duty called.

The newly discovered section of the ice caves had an ethereal beauty, with sculpted stalactites hanging from the ceiling like frozen chandeliers, casting a myriad of eerie shadows on the walls as they refracted the light from the handheld lamps. The crime scene tape fluttered gently in the frigid breeze that swept through the chamber. It was late evening, but the sun's rays would never penetrate this deep into the earth regardless.

"Have you seen anything like this before?" Ella asked, her voice echoing in the vast space. She brushed a strand of her blonde hair from her face and adjusted her suit sleeves—even at night, appearances mattered.

The two of them stood side by side, peering past the forensic techs working the scene ahead of them. Cameras flashed, taking photographs.

The light from the handheld flashlights illuminated the walls, sending streaks of color across the cramped space.

The body could be seen, illuminated by a spotlight placed on the floor, powered by a generator.

The body stood on the frozen ground, limbs twisted unnaturally in a dancer's pose—as if they were mid-pirouette. At her feet, a pool of dark red blood contrasted sharply against the pristine white of the surrounding ice, forming delicate patterns where it had begun to crystallize. The victim's skin was pale and lifeless, save for a series of angry bruises mottling her neck and shoulders.

Ella steeled herself before approaching, her breath visible in the cold air as she exhaled deeply.

"Look at the eyes," Brenner urged, pointing with a gloved finger. Ella's gaze traveled to the victim's face, where two large, golden orbs replaced what should have been human eyes. They stared unblinkingly at the ceiling, reflecting the sparse light from the surrounding icicles. Though striking, they held a cold, unnatural quality that sent a shudder down Ella's spine.

"Gold eyes... the same as the last one," she muttered, narrowing her own blue eyes in concentration. Her mind whirred as she considered the implications.

Ella approached the body, her eyes narrowing as she examined the golden orbs more closely. She reached out with a gloved hand, and Brenner handed her a penlight.

"Look at this," she said, gesturing for Brenner to take a closer look as well. "The detail in these eyes is astonishing. The size, the shape, the intricate patterns within them... They're unlike any prosthetic I've ever seen."

"Wait a minute," Brenner said, his brow furrowing with recognition. "They match Dr. Messer's photos."

"Yeah. Yeah, I think we found our eye-thief."

"Maybe our killer is a fan of her work?" Brenner suggested, still studying the golden eyes, which seemed to stare back at them from the victim's pale face.

"Perhaps," Ella said, her voice trailing off as she considered the implications. A sudden insight hit her, and her eyes widened. "Maybe the killer is not just a fan, but someone who's using Messer's taxidermy as inspiration for their murders."

"Go on," Brenner encouraged.

"Think about it," Ella said, her thoughts spilling out. "Messer was known in those conventions of hers for preserving beauty in death, turning lifeless animals into works of art. What if our killer is trying to do the same with humans? They could be attempting to elevate their victims to the status of Messer's creations, mimicking the gold eyes as a twisted tribute."

"Disturbing," Brenner murmured, the word barely audible amidst the chilling cave air.

Ella agreed, her heart pounding as the pieces of the puzzle began to fall into place. "This means that our killer is not just a random psychopath; they have an agenda, a twisted artistic vision."

"So your call on that convention tomorrow? Probably a good one."

"Yeah... yeah, I think so."

The thought sent a shiver down her spine, but it only served to fuel her determination. Ella knew she couldn't let this killer continue their gruesome work.

Ella stepped back, taking a photo of the eyes to compare it with the coroner's. She sent the attachment to Dr. Messer with the caption, *Recognize these?*

Only a few seconds passed before the reply came in.

Mine. Stolen.

Ella sighed, turning her phone to show Brenner the confirmation. As she did, she also pivoted, and she spotted a group of figures being shepherded past the mouth of the cave, rushed to waiting cars.

"Are those the tourists?" Ella asked.

Brenner nodded once. "Think they're taking them to a temporary tent for warmth."

Ella's eyes scanned the crowd of distraught tourists and staff gathered near the mouth of the ice cave. They were trying to peek in as two cops led them by. Her gaze settled on a woman in her mid-thirties, dressed in the same uniform as the deceased tour guide. The woman's dark hair was pulled back into a tight ponytail, and her eyes were rimmed with red from crying. Ella recognized her from the employee photos she'd perused on the drive over. Her sharp memory pulled the name back to mind. Lana, one of the other guides who had been working at the caves for several years.

Ella shifted her weight, relieved to turn away from the corpse. She moved out of the cave once more, treading carefully on the slick floor.

"Excuse me," Ella said, approaching Lana cautiously.

The woman paused, glancing back. One of the cops turned to intervene but spotted Ella and continued on his way, taking the rest of the tourists towards a makeshift, orange tent set up by two ambulances.

Lana hesitated but then seemed to relax as Ella flashed her badge.

Ella took a couple of steps away from the entrance to the cave, causing Lana to follow. She didn't think there was any reason to force the woman to peer into that cavern and stare at the grisly spectacle.

"Umm, hello..." Lana said.

"I'm Agent Porter. This is Marshal Gunn."

Lana nodded, wiping away a stray tear with the back of her hand. "Lana Rizzo."

"I was wondering if I could ask you a few questions. Are you warm enough?"

"Yeah... yeah, I'm fine. You kinda get used to it." She tugged at her jacket sleeve over her red uniform, shifting uncomfortably. Her breath fogged the night air.

"Do you have a few moments?" Ella asked.

A pause. A briefly bit lip. Then a sigh. "Of course, anything I can do to help catch whoever did this." Another pause. "Is it... is it really Marcy? Is she really..." A swallow. "Dead?" the word was whispered like the four-letter word it was.

"I'm afraid so."

The tour guide let out a little moan, shaking her head, and holding it in her hands.

Ella waited patiently.

Brenner shifted behind her, watching the two, but keeping silent.

Once Lana had regained her composure, Ella pressed gently. "Did you notice anything unusual about Marcy recently?

Any odd behavior or interactions with others?" Ella watched Lana's face closely for any flicker of emotion.

Lana hesitated for a moment before answering. "Well, now that you mention it, she had been acting a bit strange lately. She seemed... distracted, like she had something on her mind."

"Can you think of anyone who might have had a problem with her, or any reason someone would target her specifically?" Ella continued, making a mental note of Lana's observation.

"Truthfully, no," Lana replied, shaking her head. "She was well-liked by everyone here. We were like a family. But I do remember an odd encounter she had with a visitor a few days ago."

"Please, go on," Ella urged, her interest piqued.

"Well, there was this man on one of the tours—tall, thin, with a scruffy beard. He kept asking questions about her personally. It wasn't the usual curiosity we get from tourists; it felt more... intense. When the tour was over, I saw them talking in hushed voices near the entrance. The man left quickly after that, and Marcy seemed a bit shaken."

Ella's pulse quickened as she processed this new information. Could this be a lead to the killer? "Did you happen to get the visitor's name?" she asked.

"No," Lana replied apologetically. "But he did take one of our brochures. He might have signed the guestbook at the front desk."

"Thank you, Lana," Ella said sincerely. "You've been very helpful."

The woman gave a long sigh, her breath fogging the air. She nodded once, then hesitantly began to turn, watching Ella to see if she'd protest.

But Ella didn't stop her.

The woman moved, hastening back after the group which was now entering the tent.

Ella stood near the entrance of the ice caves, the frigid air biting at her exposed skin. She pulled out her phone and dialed the number for the local police department.

"Agent Ella Porter speaking," she said when the call connected. "I need a favor. I want you to send someone down to the ice caves to collect all the photos taken by tourists in the past week. Check the guestbook for names. We're looking for anyone who might have had an intense interest in our second victim, particularly anyone with experience in taxidermy."

"Got it, Agent," replied the officer on the other end of the line. "We'll get started right away."

"Thanks," Ella said before ending the call. She knew this was a long shot, but it was the best lead they had so far. If the killer had visited the ice caves recently, there was a chance the tourists had captured something useful on camera.

As she slipped her phone back into her pocket, it buzzed with an incoming notification. The screen displayed a reminder:

"Dinner with Maddie – 8:00 PM." Ella frowned, remembering that she'd already postponed their dinner twice before due to the demands of the case. While her dedication to solving the crime was unwavering, she hadn't seen her younger cousin in some time.

"Crap," she muttered under her breath, her mind whirring with conflicting thoughts. On one hand, she couldn't afford to lose any momentum in the investigation; on the other, it was getting late. And it would take time to gather the photos. Besides, the convention wasn't until the morning.

"Gotta go?" Brenner said.

"Might do. You good?"

"I got it. Take some time to get a warrant. Most of the tourists won't want to hand over photos. It is Alaska."

Ella smiled faintly. "It is Alaska," she mirrored.

She let out a faint sigh, then turned, moving away from the crime scene, raising her phone, and sending an urgent text.

Chapter 16

The motel key scratched against the lock, its teeth struggling to find purchase in the worn grooves. Ella sighed and tried again, the door finally giving way with a dull click. She pushed it open to reveal Maddie sprawled out on the bed, her fingers flying across her phone's screen as she typed out a message. Her eyes flicked up for a moment, making brief contact with Ella's.

"Hey," Maddie said, offering a small smile before returning her gaze to the glowing screen.

"Hi," Ella replied, closing the door behind her and dropping her bag onto the floor. She watched Maddie for a moment, taking note of the young girl's attention to her phone, her brow furrowed ever so slightly. It was no secret that Maddie had taken on the role of caregiver from a young age, looking after her father, and Ella knew that Maddie needed this break just as much as she did.

Ella hesitated, glancing at the door, then back at Maddie. "So..."

GIRL WHO FREEZES SHADOWS

"So," Maddie said, looking up and smiling.

"How'd you get in?"

Maddie blinked, glanced over, then back at her screen. "Oh... Yeah, right. Sorry. Just, you were running late."

Ella felt a jolt of guilt. She winced, nodding. "Yeah... yeah, sorry about that."

"No worries! I came in through the bathroom window. Really should lock it, Auntie Porter..." A pause, a wrinkled nose. "I mean... Cousin Porter? It seems weird to just call you Ella, you know?"

Maddie glanced over, flashing a wry grin. She had the same blue eyes and blonde hair as the Porter sisters. Her toes were wiggling in Harry Potter socks, and Ella reminded herself that one of the toes was missing due to frostbite. She had the photographic evidence to prove it, as Maddie had sent her a picture titled *Cool, huh?* from the hospital.

Maddie also now boasted a tattoo of a polar bear visible on her right arm.

Ella stared at it, remembering the bear that had chased the two of them through the wilderness during a snow storm. She shivered at the memory and felt a flash of admiration that instead of fleeing from the fear of the memory, Maddie had tattooed it on her body, as if she now owned the story rather than the fear owning her.

"Just call me Ella," she said.

"Sure. Ella. It's a really pretty name." Maddie grinned. Suddenly there was a beeping sound from the kitchen. The teenager winced, wrinkling her nose. "Sorry. Made some popcorn. Hope you don't mind."

The energetic young woman bounced off her seat and hastened to the kitchen. She returned a few seconds later with a large plastic bowl brimming with popcorn. The scent of butter and salt wafted through the small motel room.

Ella made a mental note to double check she'd locked the bathroom window.

As she thought about it, though, she felt nearly certain she had.

She sighed, deciding not to press Maddie further on her breaking and entering skills.

"Whatcha doing?" Ella asked, trying to sound casual as she sat down on the edge of the bed.

"Texting my friend back home," Maddie said, her thumbs still tapping away. "She wants to know how everything's going."

"Okay. Yeah. Well... thanks for rescheduling."

"Sure! Wanna watch a horror movie?"

Maddie glanced over, eyebrows rising high above those blue eyes.

GIRL WHO FREEZES SHADOWS

Ella swallowed briefly. She tried to hide a smirk, remembering just how much she liked adrenaline-fueled movies back in her younger years as well.

"Sure. Got something in mind?"

"*Night of the Living Dead*," Maddie replied, picking up the remote and flipping through the channels. "I think it's playing on cable tonight."

"Ooh, I love that one!" Ella exclaimed, abandoning her jacket on the nightstand and scooting closer to Maddie. "It's so creepy and campy at the same time."

Maddie beamed. "You know it?"

"Of course!"

"Haha, I didn't take you for the horror movie type. It's the campy part that makes it, though."

"Exactly," Ella agreed, settling back against the headboard as the opening credits began to roll.

She tried not to let her mind wander to the case.

They were still waiting on the compilations of tourist photographs. The convention for taxidermists was tomorrow. She had time to relax.

She *needed* to relax.

Maddie was new in Nome, and Ella knew how lonely that could be.

Their shared love of horror movies was just another point of connection for them, an escape from their often chaotic lives. And tonight, nestled in the dimly lit motel room with only the flickering images on the screen for company, it felt like a lifeline.

"I remember when I used to watch these as a kid," Maddie said, her voice barely above a whisper. "I'd stay up all night, jumping at every little sound, daring each of my friends to look out the window."

Ella smiled at the memory. "You must've had some fun friends back in Seattle."

"Yeah, and then we'd be too scared to sleep, so we'd huddle together under the covers, talking about anything and everything until the sun came up."

"Sounds nice."

"Those were the days," Maddie said wistfully, leaning her head against the backboard. She took a handful of popcorn then offered the dish to her older cousin.

As the movie played on, the two of them lost themselves in the familiar terror of shambling corpses and desperate survivors, the weight of their own fears momentarily lifted by the ones unfolding onscreen. And for a brief moment, they were just two cousins sharing a love for the macabre, bound by blood and circumstance, finding solace in each other's company.

As the horror movie reached its climactic scene, Maddie suddenly sat up straight, a mischievous glint in her eyes. "Hey, I almost forgot! Look what I got today," she said, reaching under the bed and pulling out a battered cardboard box.

Ella eyed it warily as Maddie tore off the lid, revealing an assortment of fireworks nestled amongst crumpled newspapers. "What on earth...?" she muttered, half-amused and half-concerned.

"Come on, Ella," Maddie cajoled, holding up a Roman candle with a grin. "Cilla said you used to love this stuff."

"You've been talking to Priscilla?" Ella asked, trying not to let her concern show.

Maddie dodged the question. "Let's go set them off by the water's edge. It'll be fun!"

Fun wasn't exactly at the top of Ella's priority list these days, but she could see the excitement in Maddie's eyes. She knew that her cousin needed a break from her caregiving duties, a chance to let loose and recapture some of the joy from more carefree days. And truth be told, Ella could use a bit of that herself.

Besides... fireworks in Nome were like umbrellas in Seattle.

"I dunno..." Ella said.

"Come on!" Maddie exclaimed. "Come on... please?"

Ella sighed. She had postponed a couple times, and Maddie was taking it like a champ.

"Alright," Ella conceded, pushing herself off the bed. "But we have to be careful, okay? We don't want to draw any unwanted attention."

"Of course!" Maddie agreed, already shoving the fireworks into a backpack. "Now come on, the night awaits!" With that, she bounded out the door, leaving Ella no choice but to follow.

As they made their way down the sandy path to the water's edge, the cool evening breeze sent shivers down Ella's spine. She glanced around uneasily, acutely aware of just how vulnerable they were out here, exposed and far from help if anything should happen. But Maddie was practically skipping ahead, her laughter ringing out like a beacon in the darkness.

"Okay, let's do this," Ella said, trying to shake off her apprehension as they reached the shoreline. The moon cast a silvery glow over the water, waves lapping gently at their feet. It was peaceful, almost serene, a stark contrast to the chaos that had become their lives.

"Here," Maddie handed her a sparkler, lighting it with a small lighter from her pocket.

Ella smiled as she watched the sparkler sputter to life, its brilliant tendrils of light casting dancing shadows across her face. She traced her name in the air, feeling a warmth spread through her chest that had nothing to do with the fire in her hand.

"See?" Maddie said, grinning as she lit her own sparkler. "I told you it would be fun."

"Alright, you win," Ella admitted, the tension in her shoulders easing ever so slightly. "Let's see what else you've got in that bag of tricks."

As they set off Roman candles and bottle rockets, the night sky filled with a kaleidoscope of colors, each burst of light reflecting in the girls' eyes above the waters of Nome, under the cover of the darkened sky. And for a little while, at least, they were just Ella and Maddie—two cousins stealing a moment of joy amidst the darkness that threatened to consume them.

Ella's laughter mingled with the distant crash of waves as she and Maddie prepared to light another firework. With a swift flick of her lighter, Maddie ignited the fuse, and they both stepped back, anticipation thrumming in their chests.

"Three... two... one..." Maddie counted down excitedly, her eyes widening when the rocket shot into the sky, exploding into a shower of crimson and gold. The sound echoed across the beach, a reminder of their stolen freedom.

"Amazing," Ella breathed, her heart beating fast and wild.

That was when she heard the low rumble of an engine approaching from behind. Turning her head, she spotted a black SUV crawling its way toward them on the sandy path, headlights slicing through the darkness like predatory eyes.

"Who is that?" Maddie asked, still cheerful. She was scratching at her polar bear tattoo, evidently a recent acquisition.

"Stay here," Ella instructed, her protective instincts flaring as she frowned at the ominous vehicle.

She spotted the prim, upright silhouette through the open window. The gray hair, the sharp nose.

She knew all too well what it meant—Mortimer Graves had found her.

"Is something wrong, Ella?" Maddie's face was etched with concern, and for a moment, Ella wished she could shield her cousin from the harsh reality of life in Nome.

"Everything's fine," Ella assured her, forcing a smile. "Just stay put, okay?"

Maddie nodded hesitantly, her eyes never leaving the approaching SUV.

Ella took a deep breath, steeling herself for the confrontation ahead, the scent of burnt sparklers lingering on the air.

She approached the car, frowning as she drew near, peering through the open window.

"Graves," she muttered under her breath, watching as he rolled to a stop just a few feet away. The tinted window slid down fully, revealing the man himself: Mortimer Graves, the enigmatic figure who had haunted her past and now, it seemed, her present as well.

"Evening, Ella," he said, his voice smooth as silk but carrying an edge that sent a shiver down her spine. "Fancy meeting you here."

"Cut the pleasantries," Ella snapped, feeling the weight of Maddie's worried gaze on her back. "What do you want?"

"Can't I just drop by to say hello to an old friend?" Graves asked, his lips curving into a cold smile.

"Since when did we become friends?" Ella retorted, her mind racing as she tried to figure out how to get rid of him without putting Maddie in danger.

"Fair enough," Graves conceded, his eyes flicking toward the shore where Maddie stood, watching them with wide, attentive eyes. "I'll cut to the chase, then. I found something about them."

She felt a shiver. "What?"

"I may have a line on the Architect."

Ella stared through the window. Her deal with her father came flooding back.

Ella's fists clenched at her sides, the sound of the ocean waves crashing against the shore doing nothing to soothe her nerves. She stared down at the black SUV, its glossy surface reflecting the moonlight that bathed the scene in a ghostly glow. Her resolve was as steel-like as the vehicle before her.

"Get in the car," Graves insisted, the command punctuated by the soft hum of the SUV's engine.

Ella shook her head, her determination unwavering. Maddie's safety was her top priority, and she couldn't risk involving Graves in their lives.

Graves leaned his elbow against the door frame, his gaze never leaving Ella's face. "You know as well as I do that you could use an extra pair of hands—or should I say eyes?" he said with a hint of mockery, referencing his uncanny ability to see things others couldn't. "Besides, it's just a ride. Nothing more, nothing less. We need to chat. It's time sensitive." As if he could sense her wavering, he added, "He might be in Alaska, Ella. Next week."

She stared.

"Hop in," he repeated.

Ella hesitated, feeling torn between the desire to keep Maddie safe and the need for answers that only Graves could provide. The prospect of having him involved in her life again filled her with dread, but every second she took to decide put Maddie closer to danger.

Her decision made, Ella glanced back at the shore, where Maddie stood watching the confrontation unfold. Their eyes met for a brief moment, and Ella sent her cousin a reassuring look, hoping she would understand how vital this matter was.

"Alright," Ella conceded, her voice barely audible over the crashing waves. "But this is just a ride. Nothing more. And when we're done, you stay away from me and Maddie."

Graves lifted his hands in mock surrender, flashing neat cufflinks on pressed sleeves. "As you wish," he said, his eyes gleaming with an unreadable emotion. "Your boundaries are respected."

"Maddie!" Ella called. "Hey, can you come here for a second? There's a change of plans."

Chapter 17

Maddie's eyes, wide and frightened, reflected the faint glow of the motel room light as it spilled out onto the sand. Ella swallowed hard, her heart aching at the thought of leaving her cousin alone, even if only for a brief time.

She glanced back where Mortimer had watched them leave the shore and return to the motel.

Now, Ella stood in the doorway, her cousin sitting on the bed once more.

"Promise me you'll stay put, Maddie," she said, her voice firm yet gentle. "Lock the door and don't answer it for anyone but me."

"Where are you going? Who is that?"

"Work," Ella said simply.

Maddie frowned. "We haven't finished the popcorn."

Ella felt a jolt of guilt again. She glanced at her watch. Nearly three hours spent with her cousin. And yet it didn't feel nearly long enough.

"You can sleep over," Ella said. "We can spend some time when I get back. There's ice cream in the freezer," she added.

Maddie stared. "Are you trying to bribe me?"

"A little. Yeah."

Maddie chuckled. "It's working. Fine."

"I mean it, Maddie. Please. Don't let anyone in."

"I promise," Maddie said. Her voice was confident and care-free, but the teenager clutched her phone tightly as if it were her lifeline.

Ella looked back out at the idling car.

Graves leaned against his black SUV, arms crossed over his chest, a predatory glint in his eyes as he watched the exchange. Ella could feel his impatience radiating off him like heat from sunbaked asphalt.

"Stay safe," Ella murmured, hugging Maddie one last time before reluctantly releasing her. As she turned to face Graves, she caught a glimpse of Maddie retreating into the motel room, the door clicking shut behind her.

"Are we ready?" Graves asked, his tone neutral, though his eyes never left Ella's face.

Ella nodded, feeling as if her stomach had been filled with lead. "Let's go."

GIRL WHO FREEZES SHADOWS

The engine roared to life as they pulled away from the water's edge, leaving Maddie behind in the motel. Ella clenched her fists in her lap, her nails digging crescents into her palms. The motion helped anchor her within the storm of thoughts brewing inside her head.

"Your concern for your cousin is admirable," Graves remarked, his gaze flicking briefly to the rearview mirror, watching the motel recede into the distance.

"Of course I'm concerned," Ella said, glaring at him. She wanted to snap. Wanted to yell. But instincts took over, as usual. Stubborn with a smile. That's what everyone said.

But this man was a serial killer. One she'd let go from custody...

At the time, it had seemed like a good idea.

Now, she wasn't so sure.

"How do you know she's my cousin?"

"I know more than that, Ella," he replied quietly.

"I don't want you talking about my family," she insisted, firmly. "I mean it. Please," she added.

"Fair enough," Graves conceded, a hint of sadness touching his features before it was quickly concealed behind a mask of indifference. "But I assure you, I'm here to help."

"Is that what this is?" Ella asked, her voice laced with doubt as she stared out the window, watching the world blur past in a sea of shadows and moonlight. "Help? So where is the Architect?"

"I don't know exactly, but I know two men who can find him. Two men who arrived by plane this weekend. They killed an airport attendant."

Ella stared at him. "You're serious?"

"As the grave," he replied, smirking.

Ella grimaced. "Why are they here?"

"I have a guess... But we need to confirm it. Tonight."

She stared at him, but he added nothing further.

Silence filled the SUV, heavy and suffocating, as Ella wrestled with her conflicting emotions—fear for Maddie, resentment towards Graves, and the tiniest flicker of hope that maybe, just maybe, she could trust him. She couldn't let herself be blinded by the past, not when the present demanded so much of her.

"Fine," Ella muttered finally, turning to face him. "But if anything happens to Maddie while I'm gone, I swear, Graves, you'll wish you'd never come back."

The SUV's headlights carved a path through the darkness, illuminating the deserted road ahead. The eerie silence was only broken by the occasional crunch of gravel under the tires. Ella clenched her hands into fists on her lap, feeling the thrum of the engine beneath her as her mind raced with thoughts of Maddie, alone and vulnerable.

GIRL WHO FREEZES SHADOWS

She focused on the darkness outside the window as if it held the answers to all her problems. In her mind, she could still see Maddie's trusting eyes as they drove away, the weight of responsibility heavy on her shoulders.

"At least tell me your theory about the men," Ella said. "Why are they here? And how do they know the Architect."

"They're here," said Mortimer, his tone deadpan, as if he were commenting on the weather, "because they work for him. I believe, Ella, they were sent here to kill you and everyone you love."

Chapter 18

The moon cast an eerie glow over the sprawling mansion nestled in the heart of Nome, against a backdrop of ice-tinged mountains. Midnight loomed as Ella stood with Graves beside a sentry fir tree, its branches casting twisted shadows on the snow-covered ground. The mansion's exterior was an imposing mix of stone and dark wood, with tall windows that seemed to stare back at them like unblinking eyes.

"They'll come here first," Graves muttered, his breath forming a frosty cloud in the frigid air.

"Why do you think that?" Ella asked, her voice barely above a whisper as she gazed at the grand structure that housed her estranged parents. She rubbed her gloved hands together, not only to combat the cold but also to quell her growing anxiety.

"Your parents have made some powerful enemies, Ella," he replied, his eyes scanning the grounds for any sign of movement. "Their wealth and influence make them prime targets. Plus... they share your last name." He glanced at her, then returned his attention to the mansion.

Ella couldn't help but shudder as the wind picked up, howling through the trees and chilling her to the bone. She knew Graves had a point, but the thought of the killers coming after her family—despite their strained relationship—filled her with dread.

The darkness seemed to press in on Ella and Graves, shrouding them in an almost tangible silence. The only sounds that reached their ears were the distant howling of a lone wolf and the rhythmic crunching of their boots on the snow as they shifted their weight from foot to foot, trying to stay warm. The sharp, metallic scent of the cold air filled their nostrils, mingling with the faint aroma of burning wood from the mansion's fireplace, drifting through the red brick chimney.

Graves looked out into the distance, his eyes taking in the breathtaking expanse of snow-capped mountains, their peaks illuminated by the glow of the moon. The vast, frozen landscape was punctuated by clusters of evergreen trees, their branches heavy with snow and ice. In the far distance, the Bering Sea lay still under a layer of thickening ice, the crashing waves of summer now trapped beneath its surface.

Noting his attention, Ella murmured a thought that wasn't meant for him so much as herself. "Nome has a way of making you feel small," she said quietly. "It's a stark reminder of how easily nature can swallow us whole."

"Many things can consume us," Graves replied, returning his attention to the mansion. Still watching, still vigilant, like a stone gargoyle perched beneath a steeple.

Ella nodded, unable to tear her gaze away from the rugged beauty of her hometown. As much as she had tried to leave it all behind, there was a part of her that would always be tethered to this desolate place. It was both breathtaking and terrifying, much like the situation she now found herself in.

Ella forced herself to turn away from the mesmerizing scenery, her heart pounding in her chest as she stared at the imposing structure before them. Her parents' lives were at stake, and she couldn't let her mind wander, no matter how much the Alaskan wilderness tugged at her consciousness.

Together, they stood in the darkness, alert and poised for action, as the ominous shadows continued to dance across the snow-covered ground. The beauty of Nome, Alaska at night seemed to pale in comparison to the danger that lurked just beyond their sight.

"Graves," Ella whispered, her breath forming small clouds in the frigid air. "How are you so sure they'll come tonight? What do you know that I don't?"

He hesitated for a moment before answering, his eyes scanning the dark windows of the mansion. "I've been tracking these killers for some time now. They have a pattern. They've done this before. For those who pry."

"The Collective has?"

"Yes."

"You know this for sure?"

"I do." He spoke tight-lipped, angry. There was something akin to hatred in his eyes.

Ella's mind raced as she tried to process this new information. How had Graves become entangled with these murderers? Was he hiding something from her?

"Look there!" Graves suddenly hissed in that soft, British accent of his, interrupting her thoughts.

Her gaze followed his outstretched arm, and she immediately spotted what had caught his attention. A figure, clad in black and wearing a ski-mask, moved with impressive speed and agility across the snow-covered grounds. The moonlight glinted off something metallic in their hand—a weapon, no doubt.

"They're fast," Ella muttered, her heart pounding in her ears as adrenaline surged through her veins. She couldn't help but marvel at the sheer athleticism of the masked intruder, even as fear gripped her chest. He bounded through the snow, over a low wall, scaled a fence surrounding her parents' place, then dropped into the garden, melding with shadow. All in a few motions.

"Stay close," Graves ordered, his voice tense as they crouched low behind their hiding spot. "We can't afford any mistakes."

Together, they watched as the figure advanced towards the mansion, their movements fluid and practiced. This was no amateur, Ella realized, this was someone who knew exactly what they were doing. And that made them all the more dangerous.

"Graves," she whispered, her voice barely audible as the figure drew closer to the darkened house. "You said there were *two*. Where's the second one?"

"Let's take it one step at a time," he replied, his eyes never leaving the intruder. "Focus on this one for now."

Ella nodded, her breath catching in her throat as she continued to watch the figure's progress.

Now, as if they'd rehearsed, the two of them began moving, rising from their crouch, and hastening towards the mansion.

Ella watched as the intruder's feet found purchase on the side of the mansion, scaling the frost-laden bricks with unnerving ease. Ella's eyes widened as she watched the figure leap from one icy ledge to another, their movements fluid and precise. A gust of frigid wind whipped through the air, scattering snowflakes like tiny crystals, but the figure remained undeterred.

"Who is this?" Ella breathed, her awe mingling with a steadily growing fear.

"Shh," Graves warned, his gaze locked on the intruder. His hands were tense, fingers drumming against his thigh as if itching for his weapon. They were now moving hastily up the road, approaching a gap in the fence where Graves had left a garden door unlocked.

With one final leap, the figure grabbed onto the edge of an ornate windowsill and hoisted themselves up. They paused for a moment, seemingly scanning the dark interior before slipping through the window and disappearing from sight.

"Damn it!" Ella hissed, her heart pounding in her ears. "They're inside now."

"Come on," Graves urged, grabbing her arm and leading them towards the mansion. "We need to move quickly. Watch your step," Graves warned as they navigated through the ornate garden, its statues and plants looming like silent witnesses to the unfolding events. They leaped over hedges and dodged around treacherous ice patches, their breaths forming misty clouds in the frigid air.

As they approached the entrance, Ella tried to recall the layout of the house. She hadn't set foot in the mansion since her last argument with her parents, but the memory of its grandeur and opulence was seared into her mind. The broad hallway, lined with priceless artwork, led to the cavernous living room, where her father would often entertain guests late into the night.

"Graves," Ella whispered urgently as they slipped inside the front door, "my parents' room is on the second floor, at the far end of the west wing. It'll take us too long to get there."

"Then we'll have to be faster," he replied, his voice strained with determination. "Stay close and stay quiet."

The front door had a keypad. Ella remembered the combination, entering it swiftly.

The door beeped, opening. Green lights flashing.

They moved stealthily through the shadows, their footsteps muffled by the plush carpeting as they made their way towards the grand staircase. Ella's chest tightened as she glanced at the familiar surroundings, memories of her strained relationship with her parents flooding her mind. But this wasn't the time for sentiment.

"Almost there," Graves whispered, urging her forward as they began to rush up the stairs. As they reached the top, Ella could barely make out the sound of her own breathing, her heart thundering in her chest.

"Keep your eyes peeled," he warned her, his grip on his weapon tightening as they rounded a corner.

Ella nodded, swallowing hard as they inched closer to her parents' bedroom. The last thing they needed was to be caught unawares.

Ella's hands trembled as her fingers traced the edge of the ornate balustrade, its once comforting familiarity now a cold reminder of the distance between her and her parents. The house, which had been filled with laughter and warmth during her childhood, was now shrouded in the suffocating silence of unspoken words and buried secrets.

"Graves," she whispered, her voice barely audible over the pounding of her own heart. "What about the second killer? If one is already inside, where is the other?"

Graves paused, scanning the dimly lit hallway before responding. "We'll have to stay vigilant."

GIRL WHO FREEZES SHADOWS

A chill ran down Ella's spine, and she couldn't help but wonder how much Graves was keeping from her. How did he know so much about these killers in the first place? But now wasn't the time for questions. She had to focus on saving her parents, even if it meant confronting her own demons.

"Okay," Ella said, taking a deep breath to steady herself. "Let's keep moving."

As they crept towards her parents' bedroom, Ella's mind raced, torn between the urgency of the situation and the lingering resentment that tainted her memories of this place. She thought of her mother's disapproving gaze, and her father's cold indifference as they'd become virtual strangers.

But just as they reached the hall that led to the door to her parents' bedroom, the ominous silence was shattered by the deafening echo of gunshots.

Chapter 19

Gunshots echoed like thunder, followed by the metallic clinks of empty casings hitting the hardwood floor. There was an unmistakable trembling in her hands, but Ella clenched her fist around the door handle, if only to steady them.

Gathering all her courage, she flung open the door and dove into the room, her eyes quickly adjusting to the chaos. Her father had set up a haphazard barricade behind his bed, using furniture and pillows as shields. Sweat dripped from his furrowed brow as he loaded another round into his revolver. His gaze flickered towards her, and for a moment, their eyes locked.

Ignoring his gaze, Ella scanned the room for the killer. He had taken cover behind the wall on the balcony, just outside the shattered glass doors. Broken shards glistened on the floor like jagged teeth, reflecting the pale moonlight. She could see the tip of his weapon protruding from behind the wall, waiting for the right moment to strike.

"Stay low," she whispered to her father as she crouched down and began to crawl towards the balcony. She indicated with her hand. There was no sign of her mother. She frowned for a brief flicker of a moment, wondering if her parents now slept in separate rooms. Or perhaps Lois was on one of the many business trips she so often took on behalf of the family's company.

But at least her mother was safe.

For now.

As her hands and knees pressed against the cold shards of glass, Ella's resolve strengthened. She knew that every second mattered. It was in life-or-death moments like this that she so often was able to push aside fear, to lean into the adrenaline rush. The excitement, the danger. With each movement, she came closer to the killer, her figure moving along the floor hidden by the man's own barricade. He raised his gun, sighting towards her father once more.

The cacophony of gunfire intensified, the air thick with acrid smoke and the scent of burning wood. Splinters and shards rained down around Ella as the relentless barrage chipped away at the barricade. The sound of spent shells hitting the floor created a chilling symphony that served as the backdrop to this deadly dance.

Suddenly, the killer's weapon turned. He'd spotted her.

Eyes widened behind the ski mask. She glimpsed olive skin surrounding those pools of anger.

As he moved to aim at her, Ella rolled to the side, desperately tucking herself against the wall, behind a small end table.

Bullets *thunked* off the wood above where she sheltered.

"Graves!" Ella called out, her voice quivering beneath the thunderous onslaught. She could barely hear herself, but she knew he was somewhere nearby.

"Stay down, Ella!" Graves shouted back, his voice barely audible over the din. He appeared from a side door, his eyes locked onto the killer's position. With cat-like agility, he navigated the hazardous terrain, ducking behind a toppled armoire that provided temporary cover.

"I'll try to draw his fire!" he instructed, his voice filled with determination. Ella nodded, her heart pounding in her chest like a caged bird desperate for escape. She couldn't let fear immobilize her now.

As Ella moved cautiously along the wall, still concealed from sight, moving towards the door in a crawl over glass, her thoughts raced. How did it come to this? Who was this masked assailant?

"Ready?" Graves whispered, his eyes never leaving the balcony. Ella nodded again, swallowing hard as she gripped the pistol in her hands.

With a deep breath, Graves sprang from his cover, firing several shots in quick succession towards the killer. The bullets pelted the wall, their impact throwing up plumes of dust and debris. As the killer's attention shifted to Graves, Ella seized the opportunity to edge closer to the balcony. With one last surge of adrenaline, Ella launched herself toward him.

GIRL WHO FREEZES SHADOWS

She slammed into the killer, her shoulder catching his chest. His gun went flying as he stumbled back, gasping behind his ski-mask in surprise.

She tried to snag his arm, but he was quick, shoving her back even as he stumbled against the balcony railing.

In that split second, the mansion's grand hallway doors burst open, and a pair of her father's guards rushed in, guns drawn. Their eyes widened with confusion and panic as they surveyed the chaotic scene before them.

"Stop him!" Ella screamed, but her voice was drowned out by the cacophony of gunfire. The guards, their training kicking in, assumed Graves to be one of the assailants and opened fire on him.

"Wait—no!" Ella shouted, but it was too late. Graves ducked for cover behind a decorative column, his expression a mix of shock and frustration.

"Cease fire!" Ella's father bellowed from his barricade, but his words were lost on the guards as they continued to exchange shots with Graves. In the midst of the chaos, the killer spotted an opening and bolted from his hiding spot on the balcony, launching over the railing like an expert parkour artist. He landed on the ground, fifteen feet below, rolling once, then rising back to his feet.

"Damn it!" Ella cursed under her breath, springing into action. She sprinted after the masked figure, her blonde hair whipping behind her as her legs pumped furiously.

One hand planted on the lacquered railing, she vaulted over it.

A shout caught in her throat as she tumbled, and she hit the ground, rolling once. Pain shot through her shoulder where small bits of asphalt gouged into her shoulder like teeth.

But then she reached her feet, surging up in a shower of debris.

She bolted after the killer as he rushed in the direction of the gardens.

She rounded a corner of the mansion, her eyes locked on the killer's retreating form.

"Stop!" Ella shouted, but the killer showed no sign of slowing down.

The killer raced through the isolated iron doors leading to the mansion's ornate garden, and Ella followed suit, her breath visible in the crisp Alaskan air. She blinked against the sudden brightness from the moon reflecting off the snow-covered landscape, her eyes adjusting to the stark contrast between the desolate courtyard and driveway and the frozen beauty of the gardens.

She slowed to a jog, glancing around now. Ella muttered under her breath, scanning the sprawling garden for any sign of the masked assailant. The features she had once found enchanting now seemed ominous: a pair of stone gargoyles leered at her from atop pedestals, and the surface of the once-tranquil pond was now an icy trap waiting to ensnare the unwary.

GIRL WHO FREEZES SHADOWS

The stillness unnerved her, but she refused to let fear take control. Her boots crunched on the snow as she ventured deeper into the garden, approaching the towering hedge maze that her father had imported from Europe. The evergreen walls loomed above her; even their familiar scent couldn't dispel the growing sense of dread that settled in her chest.

"Where are you?" Ella whispered, her words swallowed by the labyrinthine hedges. She knew there would be no answer, but the silence gnawed at her resolve.

With each step, the maze seemed to tighten its grip on her, confining her to a world of shadows and whispers. The soft rustle of wind through the branches set her nerves on edge, her imagination conjuring images of the killer lurking just beyond her sight.

Where was he?

She thought she heard the faint patter of footsteps.

But then only silence.

"Focus," she whispered to herself, trying to remember the layout of the maze. She had spent countless hours here as a child, exploring its twists and turns with delight. But now it felt like a foreign land—hostile and unforgiving.

A sudden rustling in the hedges caught her attention, and she spun around, heart pounding. The sound seemed to mock her, slipping away into the darkness as if carried off by the wind. Shadows now swallowed her petite form, rising around her, towering from the ground.

Another burst of sound then silence. Another flare of emotion.

"Damn it!" Ella slammed her fist against the hedge, the prickly needles biting into her skin. Determination flared within her, driving her deeper into the maze.

Ella's breaths formed ghostly tendrils in the frosty air as she stalked through the maze, her ears straining for any hint of movement. Shadows played tricks on her eyes, seemingly forming the outline of the killer one moment and dissolving into nothingness the next. A bead of sweat trickled down her temple, despite the freezing temperature.

"Where are you?" she whispered, her voice barely audible even to herself.

And then, without warning, the wall of evergreens she had been passing exploded with a flurry of crushed needles and broken branches. The killer burst forth, leaping through the hedge like a wild beast, his masked face contorted with rage. Ella barely had time to register the approaching danger before he tackled her to the ground.

The killer snarled, the words muffled by the mask covering his face. His gloved hands gripped Ella's wrists, pinning them above her head.

Ella spat, struggling against his iron grip. Her heart pounded like a jackhammer in her chest, threatening to leap out of her mouth at any second. But beneath the terror coursed an undercurrent of fury.

As if sensing her thoughts, the killer leaned closer, his masked visage mere inches from her face. "There's no one coming to save you, girl," he hissed, his breath hot and foul.

She didn't bother replying. In one swift motion, she twisted her hips, using her legs to knock the killer off balance. He grunted in surprise as they both toppled to the side, their positions reversed. Now it was Ella straddling the killer, her hands scrabbling for purchase on his throat.

"Who are you?" she demanded, her fingers tightening around the base of his mask. The killer's eyes narrowed with malicious glee, and in a blink, he had reversed their positions once more, his knees pinning Ella's arms to the ground.

"Does it really matter?" he taunted, a sick grin twisting the corners of his mouth beneath the mask. "You won't live long enough to find out."

With an almighty effort, she bucked her body upwards, momentarily dislodging the killer from his perch. As they both scrambled to their feet, Ella caught sight of the glinting blade hidden within the folds of the killer's coat.

The killer growled, lunging towards her with the knife held high.

She lashed out, catching his wrist. The knife fell.

But he moved fast, transitioning with practiced ease. As the knife tumbled, one of his hands used her momentary distraction to slip her defense and grab at her throat.

Ella's breath came in ragged gasps, her vision blurring as the killer's fingers tightened around her throat. Panic clawed at the edges of her mind, but she refused to succumb to it. She focused on the sensation of her blood pounding in her ears, using the rhythm to ground herself back into reality.

He pushed her against the hedge now, small branches cracking and snapping like wood in a campfire.

Ella's vision began to fade, black spots swimming before her eyes as she struggled to draw in air. Her lungs burned, desperate for oxygen, but still, she fought back, her thoughts racing through potential escape plans. The coldness of the frozen pond nearby seeped into her consciousness.

With a surge of motion fueled by desperation, she swung her legs upward, catching the killer off guard and using the momentum to roll them both toward the edge of the frozen pond.

She slammed her elbow into the side of the killer's head. Dazed, he loosened his grip just enough for Ella to slip free, gasping for breath as she scrambled away from him.

The killer snarled, lunging after her. But Ella was quicker, darting across the ice-slick surface of the pond. The killer hesitated, momentarily thrown by the sudden change in terrain.

But his hesitation vanished as quickly as it had appeared, and he charged after her, his movements less sure on the treacherous ice.

GIRL WHO FREEZES SHADOWS

Ella focused on staying just out of reach, her heart pounding in her chest as she anticipated his next move. With a burst of speed, he lunged at her once more, but this time, Ella was ready.

As the killer reached for her, she dropped to the ice, using her momentum to slide beneath him. The killer's fingers closed around empty air, and he stumbled, off balance. Seizing the opportunity, Ella swung her right foot up as if she were trying to bicycle kick a soccer ball.

Her foot slammed between the fork of the man's legs.

And he stumbled, letting out a gasp.

But it wasn't the reaction she'd been expecting. Nor had there been the same *resistance* to her blow she'd expected.

As the killer stumbled from her kick, she had the vague and confusing thought that perhaps he was a eunuch. The Collective, she'd been told, took their game *very* seriously.

Now, the man seemed to have had enough.

As she recovered, scrambling back to her feet, he'd disentangled and began jogging away from her.

He was breathing heavily, puffing white like a steam engine charging up a mountain pass.

He reached the other side of the pond, and then, in a few swift motions, clambered up the side of the hedge maze, launching himself over the garden wall.

And then silence.

Ella stood breathing, wincing and rubbing at her bruised skin in the cold.

She stared at where the killer had vanished.

The silence from the mansion was deafening. Had Graves been shot?

She stared at a trio of leaves still twirling from where the killer had escaped.

Part of her wanted to continue the pursuit.

But her mind kept moving back to the warning of a *second* killer.

She could just as easily wander into an ambush if she wasn't careful.

Ella let out a long sigh, wincing, and then turned on her heel, glancing back at the mansion.

The silence ate at her.

She could only hope everyone had survived the shootout and the not-so-friendly fire.

Chapter 20

The grand, wrought-iron gates creaked open as she returned, trudging back towards her father's mansion.

The giant structure loomed before her, its opulent facade marred by the aftermath of the shootout. As she walked through the front door, Ella couldn't help but marvel at the contrast between the luxurious furnishings and the desolation left in the wake of violence.

"Damn," she whispered under her breath, her eyes scanning the once pristine marble floor, now littered with shattered glass and bullet casings.

She tried to reconcile the image of her childhood home with the scene before her. The plush Persian rug that had once graced the foyer was now riddled with bullet holes.

Her eyes were drawn to the lavish chandelier, its sparkling crystals refracting the moonlight streaming in through the tall windows. It seemed almost surreal that such an elegant room could be transformed so suddenly into a battlefield. She imagined the terror that must have gripped the occupants as bullets tore through the air, shattering the peace so violently.

Evidently, the shootout had taken itself from the bedroom, through the halls.

No sign of Graves though.

With each step she took, the sickening crunch of broken glass beneath her boots served as a stark reminder of the danger that still lurked. A glint caught her eye, and she bent down to pick up a bullet casing, holding it up to the light.

She pulled out her phone and quickly typed out a text message to Brenner: 'Need your help. At father's mansion. Pick me up?'

As she awaited his response, the thought of Brenner's apartment—with its cozy furnishings and warm, comforting atmosphere—filled her heart with a mix of longing and sadness. That haven would have to wait; danger still lurked, and they had work to do.

No sign of Graves. His car wasn't in the lot, either. And there was still a second killer on the loose.

The man she'd fought had escaped.

She shook her head, exhaustion weighing heavy.

The door to the study creaked open, revealing her father standing stiffly by the window, his cold gaze fixed on Ella. A solitary beam of moonlight illuminated his face, casting shadows that deepened the lines carved by years of relentless anger and disappointment.

"Ah, finally decided to show up?" he spat out, contempt dripping from every word. His eyes bore into her like icy daggers, accusing her without a need for further explanation.

Ella's fingers dug into her palms as she tried to steady herself against the onslaught of sudden anger in her chest.

Her father hid his anger under a mask of indifference, his eyebrows lowering.

Two guards stood at his side. The same men who'd shot at Graves.

One was limping. The other had a rag pressed to a bleeding bicep.

Her father was still holding his six-shooter—his favored weapon.

He stared at Ella. "Did you kill the bastard?"

She shook her head. "He escaped."

Her father scowled at her.

She pretended as if she didn't notice. "Are you alright?"

He just sniffed, glancing back out the window. "Who was that?" he said.

"A friend of the man you wanted me to find," she replied curtly.

Her father glanced at her, quirking an eyebrow. "The Architect?"

She nodded. "They don't like meddlers, apparently."

"You could've warned me," he retorted.

"I came as quickly as I knew."

"And who was that other man?"

"A CI," she lied. "Where is he? You didn't kill him, did you?" she said, leveling her accusing gaze on the two goons.

Both men just shifted uncomfortably.

"No. He left," her father said simply. He sighed, massaging the bridge of his nose, his larger-than-life presence seeming diminished somehow in the moonlight.

She gave her father one last look. Alive. Safe.

Angry at her like usual.

She opened her mouth, paused, then said, "Might want to sleep somewhere safer tonight." Then she shrugged, turned, and began moving away once more. Glass crunched underfoot. A single bullet casing *tinkled* across the floor, sent skittering by her foot.

Her phone buzzed a second later.

She glanced down and felt a surge of relief.

Brenner.

On my way, he'd said.

GIRL WHO FREEZES SHADOWS

She allowed herself a brief smile and then left the mansion, deciding it would be warmer outside.

***

The moment Ella stepped into Brenner's apartment, she felt as if she were stepping into a completely different world. Gone were the cold, opulent surroundings of her father's mansion, replaced with the cozy warmth of an intimate sanctuary. The soft glow from a floor lamp cast a golden hue over the bare walls.

"Sorry about the mess," Brenner said, his voice tinged with embarrassment as he scooped a pile of papers off the couch to make room for Ella. "I wasn't expecting you back so soon."

"Trust me, your place is much better compared to where I just came from," Ella replied, sinking into the cushions, grateful for the comfort they provided. She couldn't help but smile at the small succulents that dotted the windowsill.

She hadn't seen them before. She wondered if they were a newer addition.

"Your text sounded urgent," Brenner began, concern etching lines across his forehead. "What happened?"

Ella hesitated for a moment, her fingers absently tracing the intricate patterns on the throw pillow beside her. "It's my father... there was a shootout at the mansion."

"God, Ella, are you okay?" Brenner asked, his eyes searching hers for any signs of injury or trauma.

"I'm not hurt, just shaken up," she admitted. "But there's still another killer out there, and I can't help but feel responsible."

"Hang on... a shootout? How? What..." He trailed off, and Brenner's blue eyes, a similar hue to hers, narrowed. His handsome features bunched into a frown. "Graves," he said.

It wasn't a question.

She didn't confirm it.

He stared at her, rubbing at his jaw with the back of his knuckles. He shook his head after a bit. "Really?" he muttered. "That asshole got you while you were on your own?"

Ella paused. Then her eyes widened. "Did you get Maddie?"

"Yeah. I saw your earlier text. She's back home. Safe."

Ella felt another weight shed from her shoulders, and she closed her eyes as she leaned back on the cushions, letting out a faint sigh.

A few seconds passed, then Brenner said, "It's not your fault you know. This shit with your family. They're the weird ones."

She forced a smile but didn't quite feel it.

She heard Brenner shift, coming closer to her. Felt the warmth of his hand against her shoulder, even as her eyes remained closed. "I mean it," he said. "They're the idiots. You're trying your best."

Ella nodded, even as doubt and fear continued to gnaw at her. "I know, but I can't shake the feeling that time is running out. And with my father breathing down my neck, it's just... a lot."

"Yeah. I get it."

Brenner sat down next to her on the couch.

A small, grateful smile tugged at the corner of Ella's mouth. It wasn't a happy smile, so much as an excuse for her features to arrange into something besides a frown.

"Thank you," she whispered, feeling the weight on her shoulders ease ever so slightly.

As they sat side by side on the couch, surrounded by the comforting warmth of Brenner's apartment, Ella couldn't help but feel a glimmer of hope amidst the chaos that threatened to consume her.

She opened her eyes now, glancing down as she did. Only then did she see the state of her clothing. Torn, dusty, and muddy from her fight with the ski-masked killer.

She wrinkled her nose.

"Oh, dammit."

"What? You hurt?"

"No. No, nothing like that." She hesitated. "You're sure Maddie's okay?"

"Yeah. I dropped her off myself. Waited until I saw her old man and heard the door lock."

Ella nodded. Graves had said that the Architect would send his killers after the people she loved.

There weren't many of those in Nome.

She glanced down at her outfit again and sighed. It was late. She needed sleep. Especially since she had that taxidermy convention in the morning. And they were still waiting on the guest book sign-ins and photographs from the tourists at the second crime scene.

But there would still be time to sleep, and she couldn't imagine going to bed streaked in dust and sweat and mud.

She sighed, pushing to her feet. "Mind if I use your shower?"

"Hmm? Yeah, sure. Go for it. Water might be tepid."

"It'll be fine."

She pushed off the couch, gave his hand a quick squeeze, and then moved towards the bathroom, her limbs heavy with exhaustion. Ella stepped into the bathroom, her thoughts still clouded with worry and fear.

She felt a wave of gratitude that Brenner's fears of tepid water weren't founded.

It didn't take long in the chilly, tiled room, after turning the shower nob, for the temperature to be just right. Steam billowed around her as the hot shower spray hit the tile floor, creating an atmosphere that felt like a cocoon, enveloping her in its embrace. She peeled off her clothes, feeling the weight of her fears momentarily lift with each garment she discarded.

"Hey," Brenner said softly, appearing in the doorway. "Mind if I join you?"

Ella looked up, her eyes meeting his, and though part of her wanted to keep her worries and pain locked away, she knew she couldn't do it alone. She nodded, letting him know he was welcome.

Brenner stepped into the shower, the water cascading down upon them both, mingling with the tension that had settled between them. They stood there, close enough to touch but separated by invisible barriers, the steam swirling around them like a silent witness to their shared memories.

"Talk to me," Brenner urged gently, his voice barely audible over the sound of the water. "Tell me what's going on inside that beautiful head of yours."

Ella hesitated, struggling to find the words to express her troubled mind. "I'm scared," she admitted finally, her voice trembling. "Scared that we won't find the second killer in time, scared about what my father is up to, scared of losing myself in this darkness. Scared we're going to find another innocent young woman... not much older than Maddie, posed like that. Killed like *that*. As if they're some animal. Their eyes gouged and turned to gold." As she spoke, the words kept tumbling faster and faster.

She felt her stomach twist into knots.

"Hey," Brenner said, cupping her face in his hands, his thumbs brushing away the tears that mingled with the droplets of water. "You're not alone in this, remember? We're going to get through this together."

As he spoke, the distance between them seemed to evaporate, and Ella found herself leaning into his touch, her body trembling with the effort it took to release the pent-up emotions she had been holding onto for so long.

"Thank you," she whispered against his chest, her words muffled by the steady beat of his heart. "For everything."

Brenner wasn't much for words. But he wrapped his arms around her, holding her like a lifeline as the water continued to pour down upon them, washing away their pain.

Ella felt the heat against her skin, the steam swirling about them like a sauna. She listened to Brenner's heartbeat as the two of them stood there, unclothed, embracing.

It was a moment of pure vulnerability, one that they both knew they couldn't take back. Ella felt Brenner's strong arms around her. In that moment, she didn't care about the taxidermy convention or the tourist photographs, all she wanted was to escape from the darkness.

She initiated the kiss. Tilting her head, her eyes half hooded as droplets of warm water clung to her eyelashes like crystalline dewdrops.

She pulled his head gently towards hers.

Brenner's lips found hers, and she felt a sudden heat surge through her body, her breath catching in her throat as she responded with equal fervor. The exhaustion seemed to lessen. The memories of the past, thoughts of the future were all replaced by the here and now.

They kissed hungrily, their mouths moving in perfect unison, dancing the way they had rekindled but also how they had before. When Brenner's hands began to wander down her back, she moaned softly, her body arching against his in silent invitation.

He lifted her up effortlessly, her legs wrapping around his waist as he pinned her against the tiled wall of the shower. Their eyes met, and she saw the intense desire burning within his gaze, a raw hunger that mirrored her own.

The connection between them ignited like a flame as they moved in perfect harmony, their bodies finding a rhythm that left them both gasping for air.

It was a moment of pure release, the worries of the outside world melting away like so much ice in the summer sun.

But Brenner suddenly withdrew.

She blinked, surprised. And then she realized why he'd stopped.

Her hands...

They were trembling.

She frowned. She hadn't even realized when the water had started to turn cold.

Tepid. She felt a flash of frustration.

Brenner still didn't say anything, moving with the same practiced, protective motions he did so often when backing her up in danger.

But now, it wasn't danger so much as the cold he wanted to protect her from.

The water ceased its cascade, leaving the remnants of their whispered confessions in the air as Brenner stepped out of the shower. He reached for a towel, gently wrapping it around her shivering shoulders, his touch lingering with tender concern. Their eyes met, and a silent understanding passed between them.

"Let's get you warmed up," Brenner suggested softly, leading her by the hand into the bedroom. The dim moonlight cast a warm glow on the rumpled sheets, inviting them to seek solace in each other's embrace. As they sat down, the world outside seemed to fade away, leaving only the two of them.

Brenner wrapped his arms around her, pulling her close, and Ella felt her body relax against his. She pressed her head against his chest, listening to the steady thump of his heartbeat, finding solace in the sound.

"I've got you," he whispered, his lips brushing against the crown of her head. "I've always got you."

Ella closed her eyes, savoring the feeling of being held in his strong arms, the weight of her worries slowly lifting from her soul.

"I don't know what I'd do without you," she murmured, her voice barely above a whisper.

"You'll never have to find out," Brenner replied firmly, his fingers tracing soothing patterns on her back.

Moments passed in silence, the two of them lost in the comfort of each other's embrace. And then Brenner shifted, cupping her face in his hands and guiding her lips to his. The kiss was gentle at first, but it quickly deepened, the two of them lost in the taste and feel of each other.

As the night wore on, their passion ebbed and flowed, but their connection never wavered. They lay entwined in each other's arms, the moonlight casting shadows across their skin.

The convention was still lurking in the back of her mind. The taxidermist was still out there. The second killer was on the loose.

But for at least these few moments, she put it all on hold.

Until tomorrow.

A sinking suspicion also niggled at her thoughts... When the morning came, the danger would only intensify.

Chapter 21

The sun had barely risen when Ella and Brenner parked their car in the near-empty lot of the taxidermy convention center. A banner reading *Wildlife Showcase* stretched across the top of the main building where the convention was being held. The morning air was crisp and cool, carrying with it the scent of preserving chemicals as they stepped out of the vehicle. Ella glanced up at the imposing building looming in front of them, its glass windows reflecting the golden hues of the sunrise. Despite the beauty of the scene before her, she couldn't shake the unsettling feeling that settled in her gut, a constant reminder of their mission.

"Are you ready for this?" Brenner asked, adjusting his flannel sleeves and smoothing down the front of his jacket. His face wore a grim expression.

Ella nodded a single time. She pulled her FBI badge from her pocket, holding it up between them like a talisman. Both of them were likely picturing the latest crime scene. The grisly murders...

Another body would weigh too heavy on Ella's conscience. No... No, they had to find something. This convention was their only lead.

Without another word, they strode towards the convention center, their footsteps echoing through the quiet morning.

As they approached the entrance, a security guard stepped forward, barring their path. "I'm sorry," he said, eyeing their attire skeptically. Ella wore a casual suit, but Brenner—who rarely played nice—was wearing an outfit similar to most laborers in Nome. "The convention doesn't open to the public until 9:00 AM."

Ella flashed her FBI badge and fixed the guard with a polite but firm smile.

The guard hesitated for a moment, taking in the badge before stepping aside and nodding towards the doors. "Of course, agents."

"Thank you," Ella said curtly, as she and Brenner stepped inside.

The convention center was dimly lit and eerily quiet, with only the faint hum of the heating system to break the silence. The rows of taxidermy displays cast long shadows across the polished floor, creating an atmosphere that sent a shiver down Ella's spine. She couldn't help but feel like they were being watched by the unblinking eyes of the mounted creatures, their frozen expressions a haunting reminder of the deaths that had brought them here.

"Let's get to work," Brenner murmured, his voice barely audible in the stillness.

Ella's eyes swept across the rows of mounted animals, each one appearing more lifelike than the last. The craftsmen had outdone themselves, and she couldn't help but admire their work, while also feeling a strange pang of sadness at all the lifeless forms. However, admiration wasn't what brought her here today. She needed answers.

"Excuse me," Ella called out to a display artist adjusting the lighting on a majestic elk.

The artist glanced over, hesitant. He had a thick beard, and his shirt matched Brenner's. The man glanced at the two of them. "Yeah?" he said, curtly.

Ella flashed her badge again, but it didn't seem to impress.

So she cut right to it. "We were wondering if any of the displays here have golden eyes."

The artist glanced at them, sizing them up before answering. "Golden eyes? They're pretty rare, but I've heard of a few collectors who like them. Gives the animals an otherworldly look, I suppose."

"Have you seen any on display here?" Brenner asked, his voice steady and professional.

"Can't say that I have," the artist replied, scratching his beard. "But you might want to check with some of the other taxidermists. They'd know better than me."

"Thank you," Ella said, though she didn't feel particularly grateful.

They continued down the convention center, stopping to speak with three more display artists and four taxidermists. Each time, they asked about the golden eyes, and each time, they received similar answers—rare, expensive, and favored by certain collectors. But none on display today.

"Seems like we're hitting a dead end," Brenner muttered, frustrated.

As he spoke, Ella noticed a table covered in photographs of various taxidermy pieces. She walked over and began flipping through the images, searching for any hint of golden eyes among the array of creatures.

Suddenly, Ella's phone vibrated. She frowned, withdrew the device, then cursed.

"What?" Brenner said.

"Those photos from the tourists at the caves."

"Nothing?"

"Not a whiff. They were busy photographing the ice, I guess..."

"What about the guestbook?"

Ella read the end of the message sent by the first-responding officers from the previous day. She shook her head as she flipped absentmindedly through the photos on the table. "Nothing."

"So this really is our only lead," Brenner murmured.

Ella didn't reply. She didn't want to give voice to the thought already echoing in her own mind.

Finding nothing in the photo book, Ella's gaze locked onto an older woman with a tight bun across the room. She wore a badge that read *organizer.*

"Let's talk to the organizer," Ella said, nodding towards the woman. "Maybe she can help us cross-reference these names with ticket details. We might be able to find something that way."

"Good idea," Brenner agreed, his eyes scanning the sparse figures in the convention hall. Mostly artists or employees setting up lighting or adjusting the displays.

As they approached the organizer, Ella tightened her grip on her badge. The organizer, taken aback by their sudden appearance, looked at them warily.

"Ma'am, we're here on official business," Ella explained, her tone firm but polite.

"Sorry, who-who are you?"

Ella tried again. "Agent Porter. This is Marshall Gunn."

"Marshall?" The woman glanced around now, frowning.

"No convicts we know of," Brenner cut in. "I'm just on an assist."

The woman with the tight bun turned back, her lips pressing in a small line. "I see," she said, suggesting she clearly didn't approve of any of this.

Ella sighed. "Ma'am, you're the organizer?"

The woman just tapped at her badge.

"We have a few questions."

"Of course," the organizer replied, her voice wavering slightly. "How can I help you?"

"We'd like a list of attendees for the event. Ticket purchases, the like."

"We don't keep names."

"Credit card history. Receipts," Brenner cut in.

She paused, frowning. "I see... And... do you happen to have a warrant?"

Brenner exchanged a look with Ella.

"Not at the moment," Ella said. "But we really don't want to put the convention on pause while we get one."

"Pause? What does that mean?" The woman wrinkled her nose.

"It means, for the safety of your customers, clients, and atten-dees, we'd have to shut the whole thing down," Brenner said casually, shrugging once. "Or..." he picked at his fingernails.

"We can do this quiet and easy. Get out of your hair before the center even opens, hopefully."

The woman sighed. Her eyes narrowed as she glanced between the two of them. But then, at last, she simply shrugged.

"I don't have time for this, agents. Fine. Come with me, please. Hurry."

Then, with a curt nod, the organizer led them to a small back room filled with stacks of paperwork and a laptop.

"Give me a moment," she said as she logged into the computer. Her fingers flew across the keys. She then stepped back, nodding at the computer. "Help yourselves. It's raw data. But I have other things to attend to."

She lingered in the doorway for a moment. "You *won't* shut us down?"

"No," Ella said quickly. "Not unless absolutely necessary."

The woman scowled, shaking her head, and muttering under her breath as she retreated back out onto the main floor.

Ella sighed, but turned back to the computer, leaning in. "Do we still have that data extraction AI?"

"Oh, that new thing?" Brenner said. "I saw it on the federal site. What we extracting?"

"Just names. None of the other information is pertinent."

Brenner nodded, and he downloaded the open pay file before uploading the same file on his phone.

Ella waited patiently as he ran the new software designed to extract names from vast text, and then hyperlink the names to DMV photos.

Ella tapped her foot impatiently. The sounds from outside seemed to be growing louder. More people were arriving.

The more witnesses, the more difficult this would become. She huffed in frustration, frowning deeply, and willing the computer to turn up something useful.

Chapter 22

Brenner connected his own phone to the convention center's Wi-Fi. "Program is already running background checks and searching their financials."

"Right," Ella replied, relieved that they were finally making progress. She watched as Brenner's fingers danced across his screen, the phone filling with data on each person.

"Here we go," he said after a few minutes of searching. "Six individuals with criminal records."

"Perfect," Ella murmured, her heart pounding in anticipation as she studied the list. "Let's see if any of them have something to hide financially."

As they dove into the financials of these six individuals, Ella couldn't help but feel a sense of urgency. Pictures on the walls displayed the items in the competition; the eyes of the taxidermy animals seemed to follow her every move, their glassy stares urging her on in their silent quest for justice.

"Look at this," Brenner said suddenly, pointing at one name on the list. "Poacher. Illegal taxidermy. And get this, assaulted a woman outside a night club after a dance."

"A dance?"

Brenner looked at her, nodding once with a significant tilt of his head.

"Could he be our man?" Ella wondered, her breath catching in her throat as they stared at the name on the screen. James Oliver.

"Only one way to find out," Brenner replied, determination flickering in his eyes.

With newfound resolve, they gathered their things and headed back out onto the convention floor.

It took them some time, scanning the figures currently working at the displays. The man in question wasn't among the artists. So they were forced to leave the main portion of the hall and enter one of the entry halls where a larger crowd was gathered, waiting for the doors to open.

"See him?" Ella whispered.

She glanced down at the phone to get a good look at the DMV photo of James Oliver. He had dull, gray eyes and a knowing smirk. He wore glasses and had pencil-thin eyebrows. He looked something like an old-school professor. If Ella had to guess, he likely smelled of mothballs.

She looked up from the photo, scanning the crowd once more. She looked for those pinched features, those penciled-on eyebrows.

Her gaze moved towards the back walls, where loners were lingering.

And then she stopped, doing a double take.

Ella's pulse quickened as she spotted the man amongst the sea of taxidermy enthusiasts. His tailored suit clung to his thin frame like a second skin, and the thick gold chain that adorned his neck glinted in the harsh convention center lights.

"Over there," she whispered to Brenner, subtly gesturing towards the man with a flick of her eyes.

"Uh oh," Brenner muttered under his breath.

"What?"

"He's not alone."

Brenner nodded past the man. And Ella realized what he meant. Standing a few steps back from the gray-faced fellow were four others, keeping a safe distance, but their eyes lingered on Mr. Oliver.

All four men were double the size of the wiry-framed, middle-aged poacher with the criminal record.

They looked like bouncers or muscle for hire. This was going to be more complicated than they had anticipated.

Ella and Brenner exchanged a look of silent agreement before they began to weave their way through the crowd, moving towards their target.

Taking in the man's expensive attire and the four imposing bodyguards who flanked him on all sides, Ella muttered, "Let's see what he's up to."

They edged closer, careful not to draw attention to themselves as they moved through the crowd. The man was engaged on his phone and speaking animatedly.

Ella noticed a small tv screen stationed above the man's table. In fact, many tables had a similar screen, all showing a similar image. She nudged Brenner, pointing at it.

Brenner glanced at the screen at the table next to James Oliver's seating and paused. It showed an image of a magnificent lion... with golden eyes that seemed to bore into Ella's soul.

Oliver was speaking rapidly into his phone. "Two thousand. Two thousand one hundred. No—no, double that!"

Ella could hear other figures also in front of screens speaking urgently into their phones as well.

"It's a bidding war," she muttered.

"Three items so far," Brenner observed, making a mental note of the other two taxidermy pieces the man had already won. Ella noticed these displayed in the corner of the screen. One looked like an otter. The other like a moose. Brenner continued in a low whisper, "All of them with those damn golden eyes."

Ella pursed her lips, her gaze never leaving the suspect. She could feel an icy shiver run down her spine as his cold, calculating eyes scanned the room, evaluating each and every person within it. The way he seemed to scrutinize everything around him reminded her all too much of her father.

Suddenly, James Oliver pumped his fist. "Yes!" he said, grinning widely and flashing a golden tooth in his mouth.

He turned to one of his bodyguards, holding a muttered conversation. And then the group of them began to move, hastening away from the screen, where a new display was being advertised.

Ella frowned, gazing after him, but then spotted a small, wooden sign over a large, loading bay door at the back of the hall. The sign simply read, "*Pick up.*"

The air in the convention center hung heavy with a mix of anticipation and the faint musk of preserved hides. Ella and Brenner wound their way through the labyrinth of displays, their eyes locked on the retreating figure of the wealthy collector and his entourage of bodyguards.

As they traversed the convention hall, the atmosphere shifted from hushed reverence to a buzzing frenzy. Through one room, Ella spotted where the auction was being live-streamed from. Crossing the threshold into the auction section felt like stepping into another world entirely—one where the creatures of the wild were replaced by eager bidders and fast-talking auctioneers. Ella could feel her heart pounding in her chest, the adrenaline of the chase coursing through her veins.

"Look," Brenner said, nodding toward the far end of the room where the collector had taken up position near a particularly striking display of birds of prey. They watched as a man in a disheveled suit approached the display, his movements erratic and his face flushed with an emotion that bordered on rage.

This newcomer was shaking his head, muttering angrily.

James Oliver's bodyguards moved to intercept, but the angry man didn't even seem to notice them.

He was shouting now, reaching out towards the display of birds.

"Hey!" the man shouted, grabbing a regal-looking eagle by the wing and yanking it roughly from its perch. "This thing's a fake! I demand my money back!" He whirled around, looking every which way as if seeking for someone to direct these demands towards.

A collective murmur echoed through the crowd as gazes were cast toward this newcomer, and two nearby employees rushed forward in an attempt to defuse the situation. But before they could intervene, the collector's bodyguards stepped in, their faces stone-cold and their intentions clear.

"Put the animal down, sir," one of the bodyguards demanded, his voice a low growl that made Ella's skin crawl.

"Back off!" the angered bidder snapped, tightening his grip on the eagle. "I've been cheated, and I won't stand for it!"

The two employees managed to corral the angry figure, guiding him away.

James Oliver watched, amused. But then, he turned away as the employees dragged off the irate man, attempting to extricate the eagle—now boasting a bent wing—from his grasp.

The tension in the auction room was suffocating, heavy with anticipation. Ella and Brenner stood near the back, their eyes fixed on the man they suspected of being involved in the case. As Mr. Oliver moved to collect his winnings behind the auction area, they exchanged a quick glance before following discreetly.

They reached a back room, cordoned off from the stage area, and hidden behind a paneled wall.

Hidden among the towering displays of taxidermy animals, they watched as the man spoke with an attendant, his bodyguards flanking him like silent shadows. The ticking of the clock on the wall seemed almost deafening as the seconds crawled by, each moment stretching into an eternity.

"Something's off," Ella whispered, her keen eyes narrowing as she studied the scene. She could feel it in her gut—an instinct honed through years of experience in the field. Brenner followed her gaze, and after a few moments, he saw it too—the flicker of recognition in the attendant's eyes, the hurried exchange of something small and gleaming. Was that gold?

Ella hesitated for a split second, weighing the risks and conse-
quences, but ultimately, with a curt nod, she stepped forward,
badge held high.

"Freeze! FBI!" she shouted. And chaos erupted.

James Oliver made a break before Ella had even finished, his
eyes wide with fright, scampering away like a rabbit-looking
creature Ella had spotted in the main hall.

"Grab him!" Brenner yelled as the man made a break for the
exit, but the bodyguards were already lunging towards the
federals. Caught off guard, Ella braced herself for impact,
feeling a surge of adrenaline as she swung her fist at the first
attacker, instinct taking over. The blow connected on the
man's nose with a gristly pop, and she immediately turned her
attention to the next threat.

"Watch your back!" Brenner warned, grappling with another
bodyguard amidst the fray. With each collision and strike,
taxidermy animals toppled from their perches, shattering into
pieces on the floor. Feathers, fur, and glass eyes littered the
ground, creating a surreal backdrop for the violent struggle
that unfolded.

"Get off him!" Ella shouted, pulling one of the guards away
from Brenner just as he was about to deliver a crushing blow.
They tumbled to the ground together, desperately fighting for
control as more animals fell around them like casualties in a
war.

As Ella finally managed to subdue her opponent, she looked
up to see Brenner locking the last bodyguard in a chokehold,

his face red with exertion. The room, once pristine and or-
derly, was now a battlefield of shattered creatures.

"Where's the suspect?" Ella panted, scanning the destruction
for any sign of the man they had been pursuing.

She frowned. The EXIT door in the back hadn't opened. The
flickering red sign above designated it and had drawn her
eye. But she hadn't seen it open. Hadn't seen Mr. Oliver run
through it.

Now, two of the bodyguards were lying on the ground, nursing
injuries.

One was cuffed at Brenner's feet. And the final one was slink-
ing away, pretending as if he wasn't involved.

Ella just let him go.

She was too busy scanning for...

There.

She spotted a figure huddled behind a toppled lion with gold-
en eyes.

She nodded at Brenner, both of them sweat-slicked, breathing
heavily.

And then she pointed.

Brenner wrinkled his nose, then his eyes widened.

The two of them hastened forward towards where the thin, frail man with the penciled-on eyebrows was cowering out of sight.

Without his bodyguards, he wasn't nearly as imposing of a figure.

"James Oliver, you're under arrest," Ella declared, her voice firm and authoritative. The man flinched, his face drained of any color, and he scrambled to his feet, his hands shaking.

"I don't know what you're talking about," he stammered, but his eyes darted towards the small, gleaming object poking out of his pocket.

Ella raised an eyebrow, pulling the object out carefully with gloved hands.

"Is this what you were exchanging with the attendant?" she asked, holding up the gold coin for him to see.

James Oliver's face twisted in anger, and he lunged forward, aiming for the coin. But Ella was too quick for him, and she sidestepped his attack. Brenner then caught the man's wrist and expertly pinned him to the ground with a swift kick.

"Get off me!" he snarled, but his eyes were unfocused, his movements desperate.

"You have the right to remain silent," Ella recited, her voice cool and professional. "Anything you say can and will be used against you in a court of law. You have the right to an attorney. If you cannot afford an attorney, one will be provided for you."

James Oliver slumped against Brenner, his body going limp.

She kept her tone cool, her expression inscrutable. But she frowned at the coin in her hand.

Gold, yes.

But an eye, no.

This man had assaulted a dancer, though. Too much to be a coincidence, wasn't it?

She frowned, shaking her head and muttering to herself. She gave a long sigh.

"Lawyer," snapped Mr. Oliver. "I want my lawyer. Now!"

Ella glanced at Brenner. At least this was a good sign. They led Mr. Oliver away, hastening back out of the convention center.

Chapter 23

Ella Porter's piercing blue eyes bored into the thin, pale-faced man sitting opposite her. His slicked-back hair and tailored suit did little to hide his nervousness as she watched his Adam's apple bob in his throat. Beside her, Brenner leaned against the wall, arms crossed, his gaze never leaving the suspect either.

"Mr. Oliver," Ella began, her voice steady and controlled, "we have reason to believe you've been purchasing animals with golden eyes. Care to explain?"

James's Rolex-adorned wrist twitched, but he remained silent, his mouth pressed into a thin line.

"Come on, Mr. Oliver," Brenner chimed in, trying a different approach. "We could make this easy for both of us if you'd just cooperate."

Ella studied James's face for any sign of cooperation, but there was none. Her mind raced, trying to piece together what drove this wealthy taxidermy collector to bid on those animals in plain sight. After further research, it had become clear that Dr. Messer's technique had caught on with some of the younger taxidermists. But was this the man who'd stolen the golden eyes from Messer's lab? The question gnawed at her, fueling her determination to break through his silence.

"Golden-eyed animals aren't exactly common," Ella said, her tone sharpening. "What's the appeal? Do you like how they look? The beauty—isn't it? Have you ever felt the desire to create something beautiful yourself?"

Her mind flashed with the images of the two women, frozen in time, trapped in those ice caves.

She felt a faint shiver tremor down her spine

"Listen, detectives," James finally spoke, his voice barely above a whisper, "I'm not saying anything until my lawyer gets here."

"Suit yourself," Brenner grumbled, pushing off the wall. "But stalling won't change the facts."

Ella's frustration simmered beneath the surface, her jaw clenched and her nails digging into her palms. She wanted answers, and the cold, windowless room seemed to press in on her as the rising storm outside howled like a wild beast. Time was running out, and they were no closer to understanding the bizarre case than when they'd started.

The wind roared outside, beating against the police station walls like an angry, relentless beast. Icy tendrils of cold crept through the cracks and seams, invading the small windowless room where Ella Porter sat across from James Oliver. The low hum of the heater did little to combat the chill that settled over her.

"Mr. Oliver," Ella began, her voice steady despite her frustration, "we can go around in circles all day, but we only want the truth. Why are you collecting these golden-eyed animals?"

James's lips curled into a tight, contemptuous smile. "I've already told you, I'm waiting for my lawyer."

In the tense silence that followed, the only sounds were the storm raging outside and the faint ticking of James's Rolex watch. Brenner Gunn shifted his weight from one foot to another, his patience wearing thin.

The door creaked open, interrupting the silence. A man in a pinstripe suit entered the room, his receding hairline glistening under the fluorescent lights. A friendly smile played on his lips as he extended a hand towards James.

"Sorry for the delay, Mr. Oliver," he said, dropping a briefcase onto the table. "Traffic's a nightmare in the storm. Now, let's see what we can do to help you."

Ella's eyes narrowed as she studied the newcomer. This lawyer had an air of confidence about him, a sense that he knew exactly how to handle situations like this. He had thinning hair and a smiling face with eyes that crinkled at the corners. He looked more like someone's doting father than a defense attorney that worked with the wealthy and the elite.

As she stared at the man, her mind wandered to *other* criminals that had means.

She thought of the Architect. Of her father's mandate to find the funder of the Collective.

She wondered how hard it was to find a lawyer that would work for someone like Mr. Porter.

She shook her head, refocusing.

"Agent Porter," the lawyer said, turning his attention to her, "I'm sure my client has already informed you that he will not be speaking without me present. I trust you've respected his rights."

"Of course," Ella replied tersely. She refused to let this man's charm disarm her.

"Very well," the lawyer continued, opening his briefcase and pulling out a stack of documents. "Now, let's get down to business. I'll need a few moments alone with my client to consult. If you don't mind." He waved dismissively at the door without looking up again.

Brenner and Ella shared a look. Then, the two of them turned to leave the client with his lawyer.

The ticking of James's Rolex only reminded Ella of what they were up against.

***

It took nearly half an hour for them to return to the room. And now Ella felt as if she were under a deluge, frustration mounting within her. The lawyer was good at his job, presenting alibis and witness statements that seemed to hold water. But Ella couldn't shake the feeling that James was hiding something, that there was more to this story than met the eye.

"Agent Porter," James's lawyer interrupted her thoughts with a polite smile, "it seems we've reached an impasse here. My client has provided ample evidence to prove his innocence, and unless you have anything new to bring to the table, I think it's time for us to be on our way."

Ella clenched her fists beneath the table, her nails digging into her palms. She couldn't let James Oliver walk away without unearthing the truth behind the golden-eyed animals.

The lawyer, Mr. Landel, flashed a quick smile, waving a statement. "Here is the event coordinator claiming she was on a call with Mr. Oliver at the time of the second murder. And here is a traffic camera showing Mr. Oliver two hours from the first crime scene."

He shrugged, sliding the pieces of evidence towards her.

She'd already seen them. Brenner was busy checking their veracity.

She shook her head. "We're looking into it."

Mr. Landel leaned back, crossing his hands over his trim abdomen. He shrugged once, crinkling the sleeves of his suit. "So why are we still here?"

She glanced at Oliver, who had maintained his silence for the last half hour. She said, "What is your interest in golden-eyed animals?"

Landel began to speak as if to cut his client off, but Oliver—bolstered in confidence by his lawyer's presence and momentum—sneered, "I don't know what you're talking about, Agent. Golden-eyed animals? Preposterous."

"Is it?" Ella challenged, leaning forward slightly. "And how about your assault charge on Donna Wilkins?"

He blinked.

She nodded, this time sliding a file of her own across. An arrest report.

Landel glanced briefly down, frowning ever so slightly and shooting a concerned look at Mr. Oliver. But as quickly as the expression came, it vanished.

Ella still wasn't sure what to make of Landel. Kind eyes and a willing smile could adorn a crocodile just as easily as a labrador.

"We have witnesses suggesting you purchased golden-eyed animals at the last two conventions," Ella said. "And you have no alibi for last night."

"What was last night?"

She thought of the theft of Dr. Messer's diluted gold but didn't volunteer the information.

Instead, she just let the silence linger.

"Then those witnesses are mistaken," James replied, maintaining his composure.

"Look," she said firmly, uncrossing her arms and resting her hands on the table. "I'm sure we can come to some sort of understanding here. If you cooperate with us, we might be able to help you out. It's not a crime to collect animals."

"I know," he said testily.

"This woman, this dancer you assaulted," Ella pivoted, "Why did you attack her?"

He glared at her. "Dancer? She wasn't a dancer." He snorted. "*Trust* me. As graceful as a brick outhouse."

"Mr. Oliver," Landel cut in quickly, flashing a disapproving frown. "My client has already answered your questions, Agent Porter. So, if you don't have anything to hold him on..." He trailed off, his eyebrows inching up.

The coldness of the police station gnawed at Ella's bones, a stark reminder of the unforgiving Alaskan winter that raged outside. The howling wind clawed at the building as if trying to wrench out the secrets hidden within these walls. She shivered involuntarily, but her gaze remained fixed on James Oliver, who seemed impervious to the chill.

She glanced at Brenner in the doorway, who gave a quick, wincing nod.

The alibis checked out.

She sighed then stood to her feet. "You're free to go, Mr. Oliver. Don't leave the state."

Oliver beamed, patting his lawyer on the arm. Landel glanced down, wrinkling his nose as if something greasy had been rubbed off.

He shot a quick look at Ella, opened his mouth, grimaced... and for a moment, it almost looked as if he were going to apologize.

She supposed not all lawyers were as awful as they seemed.

But then Landel seemed to think better of it. He held his tongue, nudged at Oliver, and whispered something in his ear.

Oliver hesitated, wrinkling his nose.

As they passed Brenner in the door, Oliver sneered, "Out of my way, asshole."

Brenner didn't budge, forcing Oliver to step around him.

Landel frowned again, but this time, the kind-eyed, smiling-faced lawyer didn't say a word.

He knew the value of taking the victories he was given. Ella thought she had the same lesson.

But now, their only suspect was exiting the station.

Oliver paused, speaking with Landel briefly. Landel gestured towards a door two from the left. The restrooms.

Brenner and Ella watched with hooded eyes as the two men made their way towards the washroom.

Brenner muttered, "Be right back."

He slipped by Ella, hastening towards the bathroom, and she watched as he retreated.

She let out a long sigh, turning back towards the mess of paperwork left on the table inside the small, windowless room.

The howling wind continued to moan outside the building.

The Rolex was gone, but the ticking sound continued to echo in her head.

Chapter 24

Ella was busy washing her hands, in more ways than one, in the female restroom, when a call came in.

She glanced down, wrinkling her nose. Brenner.

"Yeah?"

"Break room. Now."

"You okay?"

"Now," he repeated, urgently.

She frowned, drying her hands and hastening out of the wash-room, moving hastily towards the breakroom positioned on the opposite wall to the men's bathroom.

When she entered the breakroom, a strange sight confronted her.

Brenner was standing on a table, his ear pressed to a vent.

She stared.

No one else was in the room. Morning had turned to afternoon, and afternoon was quickly retreating to evening.

Through the window framing Brenner, set in the opposite wall, she watched as the snowstorm swept over the city. Large, fluttering white flakes were flurrying in the dimming light. The silent beauty of the snowstorm almost made her forget the oddity of the situation, but Brenner's frantic gestures caught her attention.

"What's going on?" she asked, a hint of uncertainty creeping into her voice.

But he held a finger to his lips quickly, eyes flashing. He shook his head, gesturing at her.

She hesitated, only briefly, but then joined him on the table.

And that's when she heard the voices.

Male, speaking animatedly.

James Oliver and his lawyer, Landel. She hadn't caught a first name for the attorney yet.

Now, she froze, stiffening like one of the icicles that had formed over the gutter just outside the window.

Oliver was saying, "I owe you a bonus. That bitch didn't know what hit her."

Brenner scowled. Ella was frowning but for other reasons. Listening to a privileged conversation between an attorney and his client was strictly illegal.

She shifted, trying to tug at Brenner's arm to pull him back, off the table. But Brenner just shook his head. "Public area," he muttered. "Their fault."

This, she knew, was a very fast and loose interpretation of the law. But things in Nome had always been done a bit... *differently.* Very much interested in the spirit rather than the letter of the law and oftentimes, neither.

She tried to speak to Brenner once more but was cut off as Landel's voice replied. "Those witness statements... I paid her the agreed-on sum."

"Good... good, good," said Oliver hurriedly. He let out a little chuckle. "And they say money doesn't buy happiness."

"You didn't... didn't do this, did you, sir?" Landel said. And his voice was hesitant now.

Brenner glanced at Ella.

Now, her curiosity was piqued enough that she didn't try to override Brenner's decision. Besides, no one was watching.

It wasn't like she hadn't broken bigger laws.

Her mind flashed back to Mortimer Graves and brought a spurt of guilt.

She grimaced.

"What are you asking me, Landel?" Oliver snapped.

"Just... that assault. You weren't strictly honest, were you? She *was* a dancer."

"Whatever, man. You knew the girl—she deserved what she got."

"Yes, sir. Just... two murder charges? This is a bit different, no?"

"You've been with me for half a decade, buddy. Don't get cold feet now." A harsh, scornful laugh.

A long sigh from Landel which echoed through the vents.

Ella's skin prickled, and she felt a chill moving along her skin.

"You didn't kill them, did you?" Landel said, more insistently.

"Look, asshole—just do your job, okay?" Oliver's voice was getting louder now. "I pay you enough, don't I?"

"Of course. Yes, but..."

"No, no buts—do your damn job!"

"It's only—"

There was a sudden *crash* and a yelp of pain.

Brenner was moving before the sound even registered to Ella.

He leapt from the table, sprinting out the door. Ella followed closely behind.

Brenner flung open the door to the bathroom and was confronted by a conspicuous scene.

Oliver was pointing his finger at his lawyer as if it were a judge's gavel, waving it about, his right hand clenched.

Landel was nursing his cheek, his nose bleeding. His faint remnants of hair were disheveled.

Brenner snarled, stepping towards Oliver, cuffs out, but Landel quickly said, "It's fine! Hey, hey, I just slipped!" He held out his hands in protection as if guarding his client.

Landel quickly rearranged his features into a forced smile and a quick nod.

Brenner scowled, glancing at Ella, but she gave a quick shake of her head where she stood in the doorway. It wasn't like they could testify they'd been listening in at the vent.

"You're sure?" she said, addressing Landel. He nodded slowly.

"Yeah... yeah, sure." He forced a quick smile, but grimaced, wiping his hand across his nose, leaving a trail of blood.

Ella shrugged, stepping back, sharing a look with Brenner.

He sighed, his chest rising and falling, and then he stepped back.

Oliver flashed a final glare. Landel adjusted his suit, and then the two men left, slipping past Brenner and out into the hall. They moved hastily towards the exit door. Oliver kept shooting glances over his shoulder as if expecting Brenner or Ella to intervene at any moment.

But there was nothing for them to do.

Ella just watched them leave.

Landel paused as the doors slid open, a gust of snow ushering into the precinct. He glanced back, frowning at Ella briefly. For a moment, it almost looked as if he wanted to say something, but then he just shrugged apologetically and stepped out, following his client into the snowstorm to where a car had been remote-started, the engine running already.

The angry glare of the car's brake lights seemed like demonic eyes in the snowstorm. Ella sighed as the door slowly shut, sealing off their only suspect.

But they didn't have enough to hold him.

Not now...

But they had good reason to keep looking.

"So, he paid the witness," Brenner muttered, also staring at the door.

"We can't bring that up."

"Could say we were told it."

"You mean lie?"

He sighed, shaking his head and rubbing a hand over his face. "Dammit."

Ella glanced at Brenner. "We could go speak with the witness in person. See if the organizer confesses to the pay-off."

Brenner tapped his nose, pointing at her. "I'll find her address. Give me a sec."

He turned, hastening back towards the interrogation room where a few files still remained behind.

Ella remained in the hall, staring through the glass out into the cold.

Chapter 25

Ella stood waiting by the main door... And that's when she saw movement in the back of Oliver's parked car. One moment, Landel had been bending over, adjusting something in the seat. The next, things became blurry.

It was hard to tell from where she was standing, the snow picking up, but Oliver seemed to bump into Landel. And then the two men disappeared behind the car.

She frowned, staring.

No one emerged.

She began to approach the door, frowning. She stepped out into the bitter cold, listening to the wail of the wind as she cautiously approached the parked vehicle.

There was no movement. No sound.

The freezing wind stung Ella's cheeks as she stepped out of the building, an icy embrace that only heightened her determination. Her breath formed ghostly clouds in front of her face as she moved cautiously towards the parked SUV, eyes darting around for any indications of a threat.

One hand strayed to her weapon, touching the gun cautiously. They were outside a police precinct for goodness sakes. What exactly did she think had happened?

"Mr. Landel? Mr. Oliver?" her voice quietly probed the evening sky.

As she approached the vehicle, the snow crunched underfoot, betraying her presence with each step. She pressed her back against the cold metal of the SUV, her heart pounding as she peered around the corner, searching for signs of danger.

"Mr. Oliver!" she whispered, hoping he'd hear her and respond. But there was nothing, just the eerie silence of the winter night, punctuated by the distant howl of the wind.

And then she saw him—not Mr. Oliver, but Landel, the attorney. He lay motionless on the ground a few feet away, his face pale and still. Panic surged through her as she rushed to his side.

"Mr. Landel?" she called softly, her voice shaking. "Can you hear me?"

Ella's hands were trembling as she reached for the attorney's wrist, feeling for a pulse—anything to cling to hope. His skin was cold, almost as cold as the snow beneath him. As her fingers brushed against his suit, she noticed dark stains spreading across the fabric; blood oozed from what appeared to be a deep gash on his forehead.

"Stay with me, Mr. Landel," Ella said firmly. "Listen to my voice!"

But Landel's stillness remained unchanged, and the sinking realization that she might be too late settled heavy in her chest. She'd seen them moving just moments before. His skin was cold, but that was explainable in the thin jacket he wore and the elements. She thought she detected a pulse, but it was hard to tell with her own numb fingers. The cold wind seemed to mock her attempts, biting at her exposed skin as if to remind her just how fragile she truly was.

"Where's Oliver?" Ella muttered, her breath forming puffs of white in the freezing air. Her heart pounded like a jackhammer as she spun around, scanning the area for any sign of him. Panic crept up her spine, making her shiver even more than the cold.

But she was alone, standing in the snow, over Landel's form. She needed to get help. She took a few hurried paces back in the direction of the precinct.

But then paused, frowning.

Was that movement over by the squad car?

She stared towards the vehicle parked between two white lines which were now being blended into the rest of the gray asphalt.

Her ears strained to catch any hint of movement, and then, there it was—the faint sound of footsteps retreating on the frozen ground. The crunching of snow beneath heavy boots seemed to echo through the desolate night, taunting her with the possibility that the killer taxidermist might be slipping away from her grasp.

"Mr. Oliver!" she shouted into the darkness, her voice cracking under the weight of urgency. The cold wind picked up, cutting through her clothes and chilling her to the bone as it whipped around her, stealing her cries and scattering them like leaves on a breeze.

She glanced back towards the precinct, turning to face the glass doors. Where was Brenner?

Still in the back.

Shit. She needed to move.

She began to move towards the doors once more.

One step.

Two.

A sound behind her.

She paused.

Another sound.

She began to turn.

Suddenly an overwhelming pain erupted from the back of her head as if her skull had been split open by a sledgehammer. She dropped her phone, her fingers going numb and her vision flickering like a faulty lightbulb.

The ground rushed up to meet her, and everything went black.

***

The first thing Ella noticed when she came to was the cold. It seeped into her bones, chilling her to the very core. She tried to move, but her muscles refused to cooperate, heavy and sluggish like they were coated with ice.

"Where...?" she whispered, her voice hoarse and weak. The room was dark, so dark that she could barely make out her own hand in front of her face. She blinked several times, trying to force her eyes to adjust to the darkness, but it made no difference. The shadows seemed to swallow any trace of light.

"Mr. Oliver? Landel?" she called out tentatively, her breath forming visible clouds in the freezing air. There was no response, only the echo of her own voice bouncing off unseen walls.

Panic began to gnaw at the edges of her mind, but Ella pushed it back, refusing to let fear take over. She needed to focus—to find a way out of this place, whatever it was.

Her fingers brushed against the cold wall, searching for anything that might give her a clue about her surroundings. Her fingertips bumped against something hard and metallic, sending a shiver up her spine.

It was a door handle. The realization hit her like a ton of bricks, and she scrambled to her feet, gripping the handle tightly. "Come on," she hissed, praying that it wouldn't be locked.

The door creaked open, revealing a dimly lit chamber beyond. Ella hesitated for a moment before stepping inside, her eyes scanning the gloom, searching for any details that might help her understand where she was and what had happened.

As her eyes adjusted to the weak light filtering through the dusty windows, she began to make out the room's disturbing contents. Rows upon rows of taxidermy creations stared back at her, their glassy eyes reflecting the pale light, giving them an eerie semblance of life. Bottles filled with embalming fluid lined the shelves, casting twisted shadows on the floor. The air reeked of formaldehyde and decay, making it difficult for Ella to breathe.

She whispered, recoiling in horror, "What is this place?"

Ella tried to take a step back, but a sudden tug around her ankle stopped her short. Looking down, she discovered a thick, iron chain secured to a metal cuff around her leg. The other end disappeared into the darkness, presumably bolted to the wall.

"Are you kidding me?" Ella muttered, yanking at the chain in frustration. Her heart raced as she realized the gravity of her situation. She was trapped, imprisoned in this house of horrors, and she had no idea how to escape.

Where was Oliver?

She felt a jolt of terror as she realized she'd been too slow to help Mr. Landel. The attorney should've stopped. Should've spoken to her.

But all too late.

A muffled shout from above caught her attention, followed by a dull thud. Her heart skipped a beat, hope flaring within her. "Oliver!" she called, her voice barely louder than a whisper, afraid of alerting her captor. "Is that you?"

Straining her ears, she listened intently, praying for some sign that someone was nearby.

But then there was the sound of footsteps. And quiet.

Her eyes were still adjusting to the dark.

She shivered, the chain securing her to the floor. She looked desperately around.

The sounds had stopped, as if someone had started moving, then found a hiding spot before going still.

What did it mean?

Her eyes moved up to the ceiling, and she stared at the wooden floorboards, a shiver moving along her spine.

Seconds ticked by. Minutes?

She couldn't tell. The silence was deafening.

Her eyes were adjusting to the dark, though... And that's when she spotted movement. There, by another door near the stairs, behind a workbench.

Her heart skipped.

But the movement was shallow, subtle. It accompanied a faint moan then silence.

She peered forward, brow furrowed.

There, on the opposite wall, she spotted a figure slumped against the cold stone, barely visible in the shadows.

She froze.

The figure wasn't moving, except for his chest. His head lolled to the side, his flyaway hair fluttering in the faint breeze of a desk fan on the workbench. And his leg was chained to the wall. It was Landel—unconscious, his face pale and covered in sweat, a chain securing him just like hers.

"Landel!" she whispered. "Hey! Are you okay?" Relief flooded her. She'd thought for sure the attorney had died.

But Oliver had brought him back... and Ella.

What did he want from them both?

She didn't think she wanted to know the answer as she glanced around at all the strange bottles and fluids and stuffed animals.

"Hey!" she whispered, more fiercely. Was he the one she'd heard moving? No... no, the sounds had come from upstairs, hadn't they?

This place was playing tricks on her ears.

"Landel!" Her voice cracked as she strained against the chain, desperate to help him, yet powerless to do so. Despair threatened to engulf her, but she refused to give in. She couldn't afford to lose hope—not now, when their lives were at stake.

"Come on, Ella," she muttered, her mind racing as she searched for a plan, any plan, that might get them out of this nightmare. Maybe... maybe if *both* of them were awake, they might have a chance.

"Please, wake up!" Ella's voice was a trembling whisper, her breath fogging in the frigid air. She clenched her fists, dragging a leg, the cold metal of her own chains biting into her ankle.

"Damn it," she muttered, feeling the weight of their situation pressing down on her like an invisible force. Fear and determination churned within her, pushing her to act even as the hopelessness threatened to overwhelm her.

"Think, think," she whispered to herself. Her hazel eyes darted around the room, scanning for anything that might help them escape, any weakness in their restraints or the walls that held them captive.

As her eyes adjusted to the dim light, she noticed the taxidermy equipment—sharp tools glinting with menace. If she could just reach one of those scalpels...

GIRL WHO FREEZES SHADOWS

Ella stretched out her leg, straining every muscle in her body as she attempted to hook her foot around the base of the table holding the tools. Sweat beaded on her forehead, her heart pounding in her chest as she inched closer.

With a surge of renewed strength born of desperation, she managed to drag the table closer, the legs scraping against the floor. The sound echoed through the room, making her wince and glance anxiously at Landel where he remained motionless.

Reaching out with her hand, she fumbled for a tool, her fingers shaking as they closed around the cold steel of a scalpel.

"Please work," she prayed, as she carefully maneuvered the blade towards the chain, her hands trembling with fear and cold. She knew time was running out; each passing second brought their captor closer to returning.

"Come on," she whispered urgently, using all her concentration to keep the scalpel steady as it scraped against the metal. Sparks flickered in the darkness, a testament to her desperate efforts.

She urged herself, her breathing ragged as she continued to saw at the chain, the scalpel slipping in her sweaty grasp. It was then that she noticed a small window near the ceiling, its edges obscured by cobwebs and grime. An egress? Possibly, if she could reach it.

As the sound of the scalpel scraping against the chain filled the room, Ella felt her resolve harden.

She gouged the scalpel into the locking mechanism, twisting and prying. It wasn't a particularly complicated lock. The teeth on cuffs, for instance, could often be manipulated if pressed by something as small as a hairpin.

Even as the thought occurred to her, she heard a sudden *click*.

The chain around her ankle fell away.

There were no more sounds from upstairs. The door near Landel remained closed. Locked, likely.

She glanced back at the window, her heart pounding. She thought she could hear music in the distance as she hastened across the floor where the bleeding attorney was chained.

Classical music, with strings and piano...

Dance music.

She felt a shiver as she remembered the way the bodies had been posed.

The music was coming from upstairs, audible now that she was nearer to the door.

And that's when Landel blinked, wincing and groaning. The gash across his head was a particularly nasty one.

The man chained to the wall blinked, looking up.

"Stay still," she whispered. "He's still upstairs."

She began gouging at the lock on his shackles with her scalpel now. "Agent... Porter?" Landel groaned. "Wha-what happened?"

"I don't know," Ella whispered frantically. "But we have to get out of here before Oliver... before he comes back."

With a final twist and tug, Landel's chain fell away, clattering to the floor. Ella helped him to his feet, her eyes darting around the room for a means of escape. The window was just so high...

The music grew louder, more frenzied. It was coming from the room upstairs, where she'd heard the footsteps earlier. Each beat echoed through the basement, making it clear that time was running out.

She hesitated, frowning at the door.

She tried the handle.

To her surprise, it turned, and the door opened with an ominous creak, revealing stone slab stairs leading up from the basement.

She felt a shiver down her spine.

She paused, glancing at the stairs then back at the dazed attorney and his blood-streaked face.

He was staring at her with panic in his eyes. His calm, cool, collected work persona had vanished in a puff of professionalism. And now, he looked like a frightened child. Ella felt a brief moment of pride on behalf of her cousin Maddie. Back in the mountains, when chased by a killer, Ella's cousin had been far more courageous.

But still, she couldn't blame the attorney too much.

"Are you okay?" she said.

He massaged at his ankle then reached up to touch his forehead, his fingers coming away with blood.

He nodded dazedly.

"Good. Come on then," she urged Landel, grabbing his arm as they made their way towards the stairs. "We have to go, now."

Landel nodded as if still in a sort of bemused trance. He kept muttering, "He... He hit me. Why did he... he hit me..."

But even in this state, he managed to stumble along at her side, following her up the stairs, their footsteps muffled by the pounding music from the room above.

As they reached the top of the stairs, the music reached a crescendo, the rhythm shaking the walls. Ella's heart raced as she approached the door at the top, her hand inching towards the handle.

She paused, listening intently. There was no sound from the other side...

She took a deep breath and pushed the door open.

It was as the door eased open that she felt a faint shiver down her spine.

She paused, hesitating only briefly as she stared into the dusty kitchen ahead of her.

A figure was sitting in a chair, facing a glowing tv where the music was blaring from.

The figure wasn't moving.

Oliver... she thought.

But she paused, standing at the top of the stairs, feeling the strangest shiver along her back.

Her instincts were screaming at her.

Something...

Something wasn't adding up.

The figure in the chair wasn't moving at all.

She approached cautiously, floorboards creaking underfoot as she extended a hand.

She should've called Brenner... should've...

She frowned. It was with a slow, dawning realization that it struck her; *this* was what was bothering her.

The call...

When they'd first arrived at the precinct the *call.*

It had taken Landel more than an hour to arrive, though, he'd been based only twenty minutes from them.

Why?

Did that make sense? When one's wealthiest client called on a murder rap, would the lawyer take a lunch break?

Ella frowned, having gone suddenly still, like an ice statue.

She pictured Landel leaning over, whispering something to Oliver on the way out of the interrogation room. Then Oliver had said something to Brenner.

Because of something his attorney had said?

Ella hesitated, still frozen in place.

She didn't reach out to touch the figure in the chair. She didn't turn around either. No sudden movements.

She could feel an itch on her shoulder blades.

And when the two men had gone to the bathroom... Landel had been the first to indicate it. As if it had been his idea, and in the restroom, he'd been egging his boss on. Almost as if he knew...

"Did you know he'd hit you?" Ella said.

She realized how odd of a question it was.

The TV continued to blare. She had to speak loudly to be heard.

There was no response from behind her.

She swallowed briefly.

And then lunged.

Instead of reaching out to touch the body, though, she surged towards the kitchen knives she'd spotted by the sink. She'd solved the case.

Almost too late.

Barely on time.

But *just* soon enough to save her own life.

She grabbed the knife.

But the whole rack came away in her hand.

Fake. A wooden replica.

She whirled around, raising it just in time to catch a knife arching towards her chest.

The attorney with the kind eyes didn't look so kindly anymore as he snarled, swiping at her.

He moved with graceful motions, in time with the blaring music, pirouetting back as she tried to smash at him with the board, sending wood chips flying.

It didn't quite make sense, did it?

But as she stumbled back, she bumped into Oliver.

The body in the chair toppled over, falling to the ground. Lifeless, a knife sticking out of his throat.

And suddenly, it made sense.

Landel had attacked Oliver by the SUV. Not the other way around. He'd struck himself and lay on the ground, waiting for Ella to arrive.

"You hid him in the car," she said simply. "You stabbed him and pushed him in. I didn't check the car because I thought he'd attacked you and run. The car wasn't moving. Why would a killer hide in a car outside a police station?" She rattled the words off, her voice shaking, but her eyes were wide as she stared at Landel.

The attorney was staring back at her, but now his lips twisted into a grin.

"I heard you upstairs," she whispered. "You saw me on a camera. Saw me come to and raced downstairs. To chain yourself? Why?"

He was still holding his knife tightly in one hand. But his other revealed a key, swinging it back and forth as if taunting her.

He didn't reply to her queries though, but instead feinted left.

She dodged.

He moved right, and she swung her large wooden board. This time, it connected, striking the side of his head and spinning him like a top.

He yelped but managed to shake it off, glaring at her.

"You were late!" she yelled, speaking louder now, if only to distract, to stall. "You didn't come right away when Oliver summoned you!"

She tried not to glance back at the dead taxidermist.

"He paid well. A means to an end. Access," snapped Landel. "Now come... I chose you for this dance. Let us dance!"

He moved towards her again, but she dodged back. He feinted, and this time she bought it, stumbling into the kitchen sink. But she swung her wooden board twice, fanning it at Landel and keeping the deranged attorney away from her.

He was now smiling, leering, even.

He seemed to realize he had her cornered, and now he was stalking back and forth like some predator.

Ella watched him warily, her heart racing as she clutched the board in her trembling hands. She couldn't let him get too close, couldn't let her guard down for even a second.

But Landel was relentless, his movements fluid and predatory as he circled around her. His eyes were wild and unblinking, fixed on her with an intensity that made her skin crawl. He stepped over Oliver's body as if it were a discarded trash bag.

"Come on, little lamb," he hissed, grinning like a madman. "Let me show you how it's done."

And then he lunged.

Ella barely managed to dodge out of the way, stumbling backward as the knife missed her by inches. She swung the board again, hard, and managed to catch him across the shoulder.

He faltered just long enough for her to make a break for it.

She raced towards the door, her heart pounding as she felt his hot breath on the back of her neck. But she was quick, and she was agile, and she managed to dart past him and back down the stairs. Racing once more into the horrible basement full of stuffed animals and embalming fluid.

At the bottom step, she stumbled, nearly falling over as she turned and saw him charging towards her with the knife raised high.

She reached out, grabbing the first thing that came to hand. A raccoon.

She flung it at Landel, and it struck his chest.

The moment the item hit the floor, though, he let out a howl like a wounded beast, as if he'd just been shot.

"Don't!" he screamed.

She stared at him. He was gasping now, frozen in place as if she'd cast a spell on him. His eyes were wide, and a jolt of sanity seemed to flash across his vision, coming in the form of fear.

Fear at where her hand lingered.

On the owl which had been next to the raccoon.

She glanced at it then back at him.

And then she snatched the owl, lifting it over her head just as he slashed at her with the knife.

"Don't! Or I smash it!" she yelled, having stumbled back again.

He froze at these words, staring forlorn at his piece of art.

The eyes above her head glinted down at her. Golden eyes with speckles of black sand.

She frowned but returned her attention to the killer.

"Put the knife down!" she demanded.

He sneered at her, his nose wrinkling. "You're a clever dancer."

"I said put it down!"

"Isn't she? Yes-yes, she is. Mother, Mother, she's breaking things!" Landel was saying. For a moment, Ella wasn't even sure if he was speaking to her. Mother? Who's Mother?

His eyes were wide, though, his nostrils flaring.

It all was now clicking into place. Landel had used his position as an attorney for Oliver to access the gold and the animals. Had used his knowledge of crime scenes to avoid being placed in tourist photos or to avoid leaving evidence at the crime scene.

He'd arrived thirty minutes late to the interrogation with his client because he'd likely been scoping out the precinct.

Or perhaps he already knew the precinct as a lawyer. Which meant he'd know that some cops liked to listen through the bathroom vents.

He'd staged it all...

But why?

And then it struck her.

Ella shivered. To lure her.

"You know... Oliver was never actually charged with that attack," said Landel softly, licking his lips feverishly.

"Wh-what?"

"The attack that pinged when you searched his financials. I did that."

She stared. And then her eyes widened. Landel had used his access to a federal database to incriminate his client. The obvious reason was now clear.

To get in the same room as her.

To draw her out in the open.

He'd gone to such great lengths... Shivers trembled down her spine now, and her eyes widened in horror at her dawning realization.

"He said you *knew* the girl," Ella whispered. "The one he attacked. You helped him, didn't you?"

"It wasn't like that!" snapped the lawyer.

"The dance hall... she was a dancer."

"It wasn't like that!" he yelled, louder, spittle flecking the air.

"What was it like?" Ella said, still shivering in the cold basement.

But he sealed his lips now. Had he been in love with the dancer? Had the assault triggered him? Or had he *caused* the assault, manipulating Oliver the way he'd manipulated all of them?

Strategists like this rarely only had one plan. He'd likely had contingencies upon contingencies. All with a single goal in mind...

To bring Ella here.

Alone.

With a dead man upstairs.

But why?

The answer was obvious. Her gaze flitted to the stuffed animals, the corpse's golden eyes.

"You don't understand it, do you?" Landel whispered, glaring at her. "You don't get my art. My mother's commands. Hmm?"

"Your mother?"

"She's always with me, you know. She never left. She was the first piece."

"The first..."

Ella trailed off, staring in horror. He beamed at her. "My first piece of art. She's upstairs. Would you like to see her?" He smirked.

She didn't reply.

Landel was nodding. He seemed to be trying to distract her, so she wouldn't break any more of his precious items.

"She was a dancer, you know," he whispered. "Beautiful in her youth. Very, very beautiful." He smiled fondly, staring off into the distance for a moment.

But Ella had heard enough.

She flung the owl at Landel.

He howled in horror, trying to catch it. But the bird smashed against the ground.

He surged toward her, screaming as he came running. Ella bolted towards a moose, half-finished, in the back of the shop. Antlers as large as she was tall. It looked to be a particularly beautiful piece.

One that Landel was likely very proud of.

She made a mental note to smash it *extra* hard.

"Don't! Bitch!" he screamed.

She felt fingers grabbing at her shirt, but they missed. She was small, but she was fast.

She felt something metal slice at her back, but it also missed. Barely.

And then she reached the moose.

But instead of slamming into it. She ducked under it. Landel hit the other side, causing it to wobble. But Ella wasn't done.

As Landel tried to scramble under the moose, Ella kicked out, catching him in his bent head and sending him tumbling back.

He'd cut his own forehead. Had he punched himself or simply aggravated Oliver to do so?

Landel screamed now. "I'm going to cut you into little pieces! I'm going to-Agh!"

The tirade was cut off by the *agh*. The *agh* was caused by the giant moose with the enormous antlers being suddenly shoved. The thing was only half finished, so the back legs were still unattached.

As Ella threw her whole body into the motion, slamming into the animal, it toppled, collapsing towards Landel with a *swooshing* sound.

He screamed.

There was a brief, split second in which he could've dived aside.

But his eyes had widened in horror, reflecting the glowing, yellow light above.

He tried to extend his arms, to catch the moose.

The giant antlers slammed into him first, then the rest of the enormous body followed.

There was a clattering sound.

A gasp.

Landel was pinned under his own creation, being crushed.

"You have the right to an..." Ella began to say, gasping as she did. But then she just shook her head. "You know what, you're under arrest, Mr. Landel."

She closed her eyes, drawing in a shaky breath, and then she retreated to where the chain on the wall still dangled. It would have to do for cuffs.

Chapter 26

Ella winced, driving in the rear of the convoy of emergency vehicles heading back to Nome.

The mountains were in her rearview mirror. And the ambulance behind her was flanked by four police cars.

Landel wasn't going anywhere.

She allowed herself a small, tired smile, her hands gripping the steering wheel as she moved along the icy roads.

The blizzard was quieting but had left its snowy burden along the ground.

Ella sighed. In the end, Landel had seemed almost relieved to be arrested, though, she hadn't asked him why.

Most likely, the trial wouldn't shed much light on what he'd been planning; she couldn't help but feel like draining the swamp had only led to more muck and mire.

But at least the pieces were moving into place.

She picked up the speed, ignoring the ice under her tires.

She pulled out ahead of the slower emergency vehicles behind her, moving fast.

She felt her lips turn into a faint smile.

She liked driving on ice. Liked the danger of it. The *rush*.

She floored the pedal, moving even faster.

Brenner would've chastised her. She chuckled.

But then frowned.

Brenner hadn't come. She'd looked for him among the emergency vehicles. But he hadn't been at the scene.

Perhaps he'd gone home, assuming she'd left?

Maybe he was asleep...

She frowned, wondering why this bothered her.

Her mind seemed to drift as she continued to speed away.

Landel was in custody. The killer was caught.

But her sense of unease still lingered.

Her father's demands to find the Architect were still fresh in her mind. The threat of her family was still very much present.

She couldn't forget the Collective, and Mortimer Graves' help back at her father's mansion. The Graveyard Killer was still out there, still somehow... an ally and a threat at the same time.

She let out another, longer sigh.

And that's when her phone began to ring.

She paused, glancing at the seat next to her.

The phone buzzed again.

She stared.

Brenner's number.

She grinned, feeling a surge of relief.

"Hey, jerk. Could've at least come and said hi," she said in a playful, teasing voice. She pressed the cold phone against her cheek. "Don't worry. I'm fine," she added.

Brenner didn't speak. For a moment, there was only heavy breathing on the line. Someone listening.

No... no, not someone.

More than one person breathing.

Two someones.

Two.

Where was the second killer?

"Ella Porter?" said a dull voice.

"Who is this?"

Her grin vanished like snow in sunlight. A sudden burst of fear spread through her body as if she'd been wrapped in a warm blanket.

"Ella Porter?"

"Brenner? Where is he! Where's Gunn?" Her voice was shaking and shrill to her own ears.

She swallowed and cursed as she was forced to veer back onto the road, kicking up a cloud of ice.

She couldn't slow, though. Her worst fears were now coming true.

"You want to see him alive again? Come to us. No cops."

"Where are you?" she said, her voice hoarse. "Who is this?"

"I'm texting the address. Come right now. Or I'll cut him to pieces and mail them to you."

He said it so matter-of-factly, as if he were simply commenting on the weather.

"Wait!" she said, panic flaring, sensing the imminent end of the conversation.

But then, the voice gave an indifferent grunt and hung up.

She heard only dead air for a moment, speeding through the snow, kicking up tufts of ice crystals.

And then her phone screen blinked.

GIRL WHO FREEZES SHADOWS

A text message coming in.

The address for Brenner's apartment.

To say she floored it would've been a gross understatement. The car had likely never gone so fast, certainly not in such conditions.

But nothing could slow her, panic filling every pore as she raced back towards town, back towards Brenner's apartment, fearing the worst had already happened.

What's Next for Ella Porter?

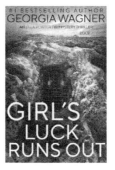

Ghosts may never die, but the girls found in the Kennicott Ghost Town aren't so lucky...

And luck is the killer's MO. He plays games of chance with his victims. Some are released if they win, but others are forced to go all-in. Poker chips, dice, lottery slips are left in the hands of the deceased as a taunting reminder of the killer's cruel designs.

GIRL WHO FREEZES SHADOWS

High-profile victims are showing up in the abandoned
Alaskan town, amidst the desolate buildings and old copper
mineshafts. The daughter of a mayor, the wife of a police
chief—the killer seems to be escalating.

Agent Ella Porter finds herself entangled in a deadly
cat-and-mouse game with a cunning killer. As bodies begin
to pile up, thrown down old copper mineshafts, Ella races
against time to solve the case before more lives are claimed.

But following a shocking revelation of blackmail, and months
of secrecy, Ella realizes the case isn't at all what she first
thought.

As Ella delves deeper into the twisted psyche of the killer,
she unearths a haunting history that connects the present-day
crimes to the forgotten past of the ghost town.

Other Books by Georgia Wagner

The skeletons in her closet are twitching...

Genius chess master and FBI consultant Artemis Blythe swore she'd never return to the misty Cascade Mountains.Her father—a notorious serial killer, responsible for the deaths of seven women—is now imprisoned, in no small part due to a clue she provided nearly fifteen years ago.And now her father wants his vengeance.

GIRL WHO FREEZES SHADOWS

A new serial killer is hunting the wealthy and the elite in the town of Pinelake. Artemis' father claims he knows the identity of the killer, but he'll only tell daughter dearest. Against her will, she finds herself forced back to her old stomping grounds.

Once known as a child chess prodigy, now the locals only think of her as 'The Ghostkiller's' daughter.In the face of a shamed family name and a brother involved with the Seattle mob, Artemis endeavors to use her tactical genius to solve the baffling case.

Hunting a murderer who strikes without a trace, if she fails, the next skeleton in her closet will be her own.

Other Books by Georgia Wagner

A cold knife, a brutal laugh. Then the odds-defying escape.

Once a hypnotist with her own TV show, now, Sophie Quinn works as a full-time consultant for the FBI. Everything changed six years ago. She can still remember that horrible night. Slated to be the River Killer's tenth victim, she managed to slip her bindings and barely escape where so many others failed. Her sister wasn't so lucky.

GIRL WHO FREEZES SHADOWS

And now the killer is back.

Two PHDs later, she's now a rising star at the FBI. Her photographic memory helps solve crimes, but also helps her to never forget. She saw the River Killer's tattoo. She knows what he sounds like. And now, ten years later, he's active again.

Sophie Quinn heads back home to the swamps of Louisiana, along the Mississippi River, intent on evening the score and finding the man who killed her sister. It's been six years since she's been home, though. Broken relationships and shattered dreams exist among the bayous, the rivers, the waterways and swamps of Louisiana; can Sophie find her way home again? Or will she be the River Killer's next victim to float downstream?

Want to know more?

Greenfield press is the brainchild of bestselling author Steve Higgs. He specializes in writing fast paced adventurous mystery and urban fantasy with a humorous lilt. Having made his money publishing his own work, Steve went looking for a few 'special' authors whose work he believed in.

Georgia Wagner was the first of those, but to find out more and to be the first to hear about new releases and what is coming next, you can join the Facebook group by copying the following link into your browser - www.facebook.com/Gree nfieldPress.

About the Author

Georgia Wagner worked as a ghost writer for many, many years before finally taking the plunge into self-publishing. Location and character are two big factors for Georgia, and getting those right allows the story to flow seamlessly onto the page. And flow it does, because Georgia is so prolific a new term is required to describe the rate at which nerve-tingling stories find their way into print.

When not found attached to a laptop, Georgia likes spending time in local arboretums, among the trees and ponds. An avid cultivator of orchids, begonias, and all things floral, Georgia also has a strong penchant for art, paintings, and sculptures. A many-decades long passion for mystery novels.

Printed in Great Britain
by Amazon

29568075R00155